WITCH WAY TO DEATH & DESTRUCTION

THE WITCH WAY MYSTERIES - BOOK 5

JANE HINCHEY

BP
BAYWOLF PRESS

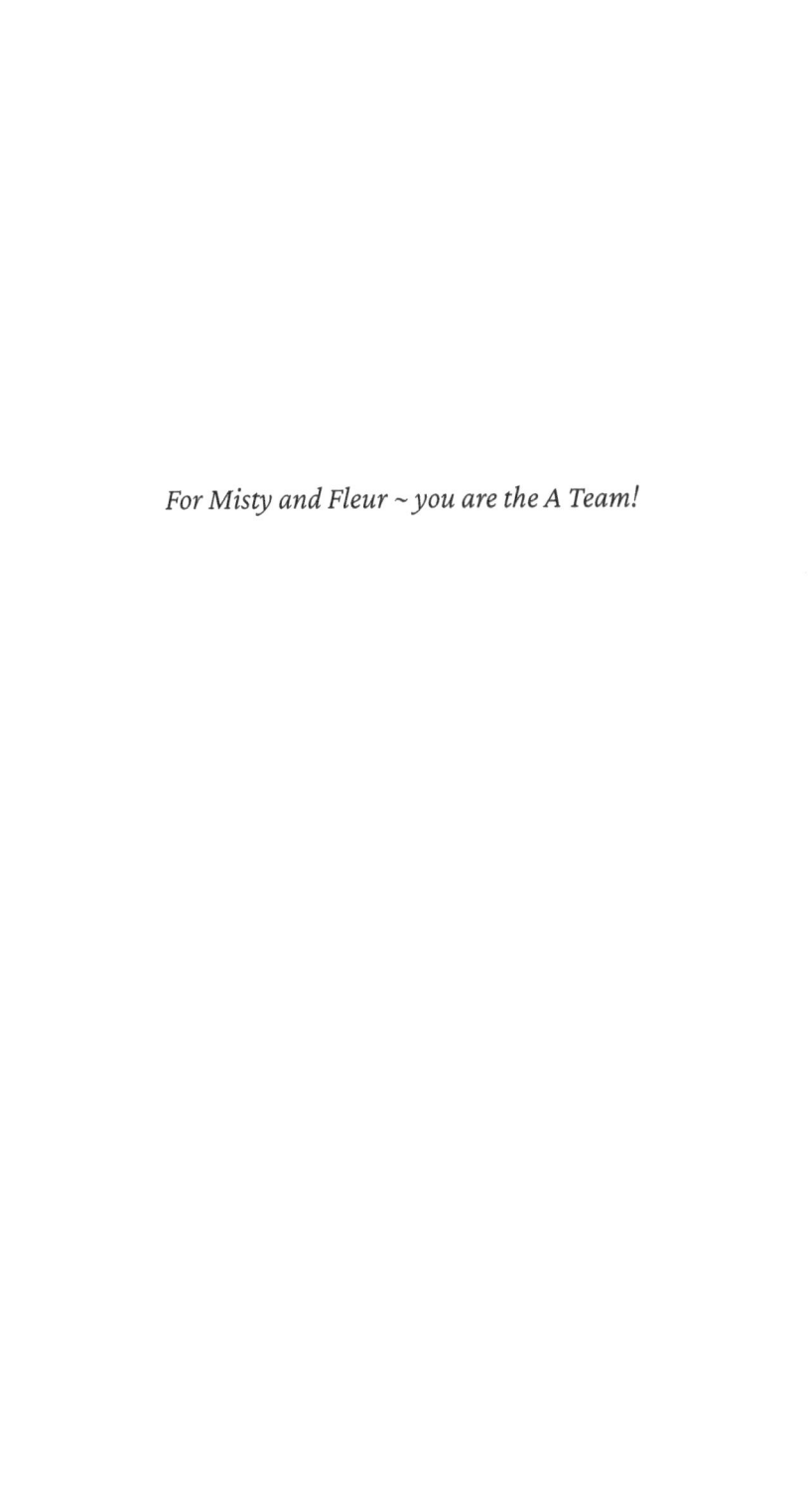

For Misty and Fleur ~ you are the A Team!

AUTHOR'S NOTE

Hey there! Welcome to a whirlwind of whimsy and wonder in my Witch Way Mysteries. If you've got a soft spot for the supernatural, you're in for a real treat.

This is your gateway to a world where magic and mystery intertwine. The Witch Way series has now woven its full tale, but the magic doesn't stop here. For news on my latest adventures and stories, don't forget to sign up for my newsletter.

Janehinchey.com/subscribe

Are you ready to conjure up some fun and unravel a few bewitching puzzles? I'll see you on the other side!

xoxo
Jane

ABOUT THIS BOOK

A druid, a sorceress, and a demon hunter walk into a bar... sounds like the start of a joke, right? Only it's no joke. Whitefall Cove is overrun with otherworld creatures and this trio is our only hope.

With townsfolk possessed and goblins running amok, the last thing we need is a murder, but someone is out for blood, and I fear it's mine. Llewellyn the demon hunter is convinced I'm some powerful witch that needs protecting, and as more and more bizarre occurrences pile up, I'm starting to think he might be right.

Can the supernatural threesome free our town from the grip of terror the demons have wrought, or will the darkness that I can sense coming—the one that is creeping closer and has eyes that glow red in the night—finally be my undoing?

This paranormal murder mystery will have you completely spellbound and laughing out loud!

CHAPTER

ONE

"There is a demon on the loose in Whitefall Cove."

A startled gasp echoed through the room, followed by murmurs and whispering. I glanced at Gran who was seated next to me in a black satin ball gown complete with top hat, then turned my attention back to Izzy who'd called this emergency meeting. Esmerelda Higgingbottom—Izzy for short—was the headmistress of Drixworths Academy of Witchcraft and Wizardry, where young witches and warlocks study the craft before obtaining their witches license, and it was in one of her classrooms where we now sat.

"How did this happen?" Poppy and Hetty Oliver said in unison. "We thought this town was safe!" The two sisters ran a tea shop along the esplanade called

The Tea Leaf. Poppy and Hetty weren't twins, but they could have been. A year apart in age—somewhere in their fifties—and dressed eerily similar. Floral dresses, sensible shoes, short, curly hair, pearl necklaces.

Izzy nodded. "It is true, our ancestors warded the township hundreds of years ago to create a haven for supernaturals and humans alike. But those wards have been broken."

"But how?" Poppy was genuinely puzzled. "If they were powerful wards, designed to last many lifetimes, how could they have been broken? And by whom?"

"Yes," Hetty added. "We specifically chose to move to Whitefall Cove because of its non-demon rating. This is most disappointing." She huffed, arms crossed, mouth downturned.

Izzy smiled gently at the two women. "I agree, it is of great concern. That's why I have invited both a sorceress and a druid to assist us with re-establishing the wards and banishing any demons."

"You're sure a demon has gotten past the wards?" I asked, curious, along with everyone else, that one-day Whitefall Cove was its usual idyllic haven and the next we had a demon problem.

"There has been a possession, yes," Izzy confirmed. A ruckus broke out, everyone talking over each other, voices rising as panic swept through the room.

"It's not some prankster fooling around, is it?" A voice boomed from the back.

Gran stiffened next to me and I pinned her with a look.

"What?" she hissed. "It isn't me, I swear. Although it does give me ideas." She tapped her lip thoughtfully.

"Gran!" I warned. I wouldn't put it past her to pull such tricks, but I also knew if she said she wasn't responsible, she wasn't. Gran liked to take full credit for her endeavors. Plus, possessing someone took a lot of power. I doubted if any of the witches in Whitefall Cove had the ability.

Jackson, who was seated on the other side of me, raised his hand. "If I may, Izzy?" Jackson was a necromancer and as such he had a close relationship with the spirit world and could often see and communicate with ghosts.

"Jackson." Izzy nodded and he rose to his feet, addressing the room.

"I think Izzy is right—whether it's a demon or something else, there is something amiss in Whitefall Cove. The ghosts are...panicked. Agitated."

"Do you know why?" I asked, surprised he'd never mentioned this to me before.

"They've stopped speaking to me," he replied, glancing down at me. "Whenever I approach, they vaporize."

"Sounds to me like they're scared of you." Poppy sniffed. I swiveled to frown at her. Jackson had a very

3

good relationship with the ghosts—they had nothing to fear from him and they knew it.

"Maybe they're avoiding him because they're scared he will ask them what's going on?" I said in his defense. "Maybe the ghosts know about the demon and that's what's got them rattled."

"Possibly," Izzy agreed.

"Why didn't you tell me this before?" I whispered when Jackson sat back down.

He placed a hand on my knee and squeezed. "We've always had more interesting things to talk about." He grinned. It was true. Jackson and I had been dating for a few weeks now and our time together had been spent doing much more romantic things, like candlelight dinners, walks on the beach, stuff straight out of a romantic movie. Gran said it made her want to puke, but I'd seen the teasing gleam in her eye and knew she was beyond happy for us.

"As I said," Izzy continued, "a sorceress and druid are on hand to assist us. Please join me in welcoming sorceress, Morgan Healy."

Heads swiveled as a woman at the back of the room stood. She was drop-dead gorgeous and, judging by the stunned silence, I wasn't the only one who thought so. With tanned skin, winged eyeliner accentuating dark eyes and Icelandic white hair, it was a combination not to be missed. Add in the white bustier hugging her petite figure, long white nails, and a tribal tattoo that wrapped around her wrist, across the back of her hand and up her thumb and forefinger, she projected an overall badass vibe.

"Wowee," Gran declared. I could see the cogs turning in her head, planning on how she could emulate Morgan's look. We all watched, mesmerized, as Morgan moved to the front of the room. I cocked my head, studying her. She looked like she wasn't walking at all, yet her body was moving and I wondered if she were floating. Her long skirt hid her feet from view so I wasn't one hundred percent sure if she just moved with the utmost grace or if sorcery was involved.

"Thank you, Izzy." Morgan's voice was as seductive as her appearance, warm and husky, and we all sat with bated breath, fully prepared to hang on her every word. "I'm delighted to be here. Whitefall Cove is a beautiful town."

"Yeah, if you don't count the demon," Gran grumbled, crossing her arms over her chest, a frown pulling her brows tight. I glanced at Jackson, who quirked an eyebrow. Gran had that look about her, the one that said she was ready for a fight, and when Gran was in that mood she was like a dog with a bone. Morgan had better have some satisfactory answers.

"That is so." Morgan inclined her head in Gran's direction, then lifted one arm gracefully, and as if in slow motion, flicked her waist-length hair over one shoulder. I swear to God I saw gold dust sparkle in the air. Gran relaxed back in her seat, hands falling into her lap. Had Morgan done something with that fairy dust? Or had it all been an illusion? I felt a bit muddled, and Gran was strangely unanimated. For Gran, that is.

Morgan lifted both arms out from her sides, closed her eyes and tilted her head back. "I sense multiple creatures," she breathed, "but they are nothing. A trifling nuisance, easily dealt with. Something worse is coming. Something dark. Something evil."

We gasped, horrified.

"What is it?" Izzy asked. "What do you see?"

"Something dark is coming this way," Morgan repeated, lowering her arms and opening her eyes.

"Really, Morgan? That's the best you've got?" Heads swiveled to the voice coming from the doorway. He was a giant of a man, his dark head brushing the top of the doorframe, his broad shoulders touching each side. As much as Morgan had an ethereal beauty, this man had a commanding presence, not so much in his looks, that, when pressed you'd say were quite ordinary, but he had a magnetic quality. He was the type of man that men wanted to be, and women wanted to be with.

Izzy beckoned him forward. "Please meet Finn Hurley. Finn is a druid and he joins us from the Otherworld."

My mouth dropped open. I'd heard about the

Otherworld but had thought it was the stuff of fairytales. I'd never believed it actually existed.

Finn stepped into the room and mist swirled around his feet as he moved.

"Thank you for inviting me, Izzy." He gave a slight bow and heat colored Izzy's cheeks. I sighed. Finn nodded at Morgan who so far had refused to acknowledge him. I wondered if the two of them had history, the way she stood rigidly ignoring him made me think they were familiar with each other.

"Here's how I see it, folks." Finn addressed us and the room hung on his word much as it had Morgan's. "Whitefall Cove is a special place. A magical town. And for good reason. It started as a conduit between worlds. A way for beings to travel from one dimension to another. Then the war came, allegiances were forged, and the portal closed. It's been that way for millennia."

"Until now," Morgan drawled, studying her nails.

Finn inclined his head. "Agreed. Until now. But, and you'll have to take my word for this as a seer and a druid, there is nothing sinister in it. Yes, the wards have been breached and they will be restored. Morgan and I will see to it."

"How can you say it's not sinister?" Jackson said. "Something powerful broke those wards, wards that have withheld attacks for, I presume, hundreds of years. Why now?"

"Whitefall Cove is built where the veil between dimensions is thin." Morgan pinned Jackson with her dark gaze and he audibly swallowed. "Making it an attractive target. But also, a forgotten one. Who here knew of this? Knew of Whitefall Cove's beginnings?"

We all looked at each other in confusion. I'd had no idea. It seemed neither did anyone else.

"I believe the wards were broken by accident." Finn folded his thick arms across his chest. "They weren't deliberately broken, it was fallout from some other activity."

"And we're here to discover what." Morgan nodded, moving to stand united with Finn. "For the magic that broke the wards? Was dark."

"You're saying black magic?" Hetty Oliver squeaked, aghast at the very idea.

"Isn't that illegal?" Poppy looked from her sister to the trio holding court in the front of the room.

"Correct on both counts." Izzy nodded. She turned her attention to Finn and Morgan. "I should let you know that I've also invited someone else to assist us in our time of need." She glanced at her watch. "I was hoping he'd be here by now, but he must have been held up."

"He?" Morgan tossed her hair over one shoulder in apparent interest at the mention of another male. Finn crossed his arms over his chest and frowned.

"Yes," Izzy said. "A demon hunter. We need this situation dealt with quickly and efficiently."

Morgan and Finn snorted in perfect unison.

"I assure you, we can take care of it," Finn said.

Izzy arched one perfectly manicured eyebrow at him. "I'm sure you can. I'm also sure you'll agree that your time, not to mention your skills and talents, would be best spent repairing the wards and getting to the bottom of how they were broken. Chasing down any creatures that have found their way here shouldn't distract you from your task."

"Who is the demon hunter, may I ask?" Morgan asked while Finn floundered for a response to Izzy's words.

"Llewellyn Cox," Izzy said. "You know of him?"

"I've heard of him, yes, but have not crossed paths with him before." She inclined her head as if giving a nod of approval.

Izzy turned to the audience. "I know this has been a shock. We've lived a peaceful existence here for so long that the thought of demons, or any otherworldly creature for that matter, infiltrating Whitefall Cove wanting to do harm is difficult to fathom. But we're taking care of it, as you can see." She indicated Finn and Morgan by her side. "I urge you now not to panic. Be mindful, if you see a demon, or come across evidence of one, please let us know."

"What signs should we be looking for?" Poppy asked, wringing her hands in anguish.

"Anything out of the ordinary. Strange noises. The smell of sulfur. Mysterious shadows. Anything odd. Don't hesitate. Call any one of us. And as soon as Llewellyn arrives I'll hand out his number and you can call him direct—he'll be dealing with any creatures that have crossed over into this dimension. Do not, under any circumstances, approach a demon on your own. Call for help. Understood?"

Heads nodded grimly. With Gran on one side of me and Jackson on the other, I held both their hands and squeezed, an unsettling sensation wrapping itself around me that I just couldn't shake. Maybe it was the thrum of magic in the room from the presence of Finn and Morgan, or maybe it was something more sinister...I just didn't know, and I certainly didn't like it.

CHAPTER

TWO

"A demon is on the loose in Whitefall Cove." The words reverberated through my head as soft as a whisper yet so loud they hurt my ears.

I jolted awake, body bathed in sweat. Outside, the wind howled and a branch of the old oak tree next to my cottage tapped insistently on the side of the house. Sitting up, I pushed the covers away, tugging at the tank that now clung to my damp skin.

"*Mreeeow?*" Archie lifted his head from the foot of the bed, his sleepy eyes regarding me.

"It's okay," I reassured him, swinging my legs over the edge of the bed and letting the night air cool my overheated senses. I sat for long moments, letting the night swarm around me. It was quiet here in the lighthouse cottage. We were on the bluff, isolated from the town. Usually, I liked it, but tonight? Tonight I'd given myself the heebie-jeebies, especially after all the talk of demons and broken wards at the meeting earlier.

"I'm just going to strengthen the wards," I told Archie. He wasn't just my cat, he was my familiar, and despite Gran saying he spoke to her, I'd yet to understand a word from him. To me, he was all meows, purrs, and the occasional growl if I scratched his belly that millisecond too long.

Archie had been sliding back into sleep, but at this, his eyes sprang open and he sat up, instantly alert. Jumping off the bed, he disappeared into the hallway and I heard a creak as his paws found the squeaky tread on the way downstairs.

I followed, cursing when I flicked the light switch only to have nothing happen. The power must be out. The wind howled again and if the cottage had been built from anything other than the strongest of stone I'm sure it would have shuddered under the onslaught. As it was, it didn't move. Just the *tap, tap, tap* of the tree outside. Holding out my hand, I summoned a light ball to guide the way, balancing it on my palm as I made my way downstairs. With a snap of my fingers, the candles around my living and dining room flared to life.

Archie was in the kitchen, crunching on the kibble in his bowl. "And here I thought you rushed downstairs to protect me." I chuckled. When we'd moved into the caretaker's cottage, my coven had turned up to cleanse and ward my new home, with the reminder to keep the wards topped up or they could, and would, fail.

"I know it's probably my over-reactive imagination," I continued, speaking to my cat who still had his face buried in his food bowl, "but ever since Morgan and Finn turned up I've been on edge. I mean, a sorceress and druid, here, in Whitefall Cove? Absurd." I crossed to the front door, pressed my ear to it, as if I'd hear a demon creeping about on the other side, before laughing softly to myself and cautiously opening the door.

The wind hit me in the face. I staggered, grasping the door to brace myself against the onslaught. Standing in the doorway, I placed my palm against the sigil marking the ward and closed my eyes, reciting the spell to keep evil out of my home. Opening my eyes, I sucked in a startled breath. There! On the dirt track that led up to the lighthouse, in the total and utter darkness of the night, two red eyes blinked at me.

With a squeal I slammed the door shut, throwing the bolt across, my heart pounding so frantically in my chest I could hear it echoing in my ears. I sprinted to the back door. I had to strengthen that ward too and then we'd be safe. *Tap, tap, tap* went the tree outside. This time a gust of wind so powerful hit that the house groaned. This house never groaned. It was a solid fortress designed to withstand anything the weather could toss at it. Flinging open the back door, I stepped outside, raised my hand and placed it on top of the sigil, repeating the process. It wasn't until it was done, the door shut and bolted, that I released the breath I didn't realize I'd been holding, feeling just a tad lightheaded.

"Oh God," I whispered, dragging myself to the sofa and sitting with my head cradled in my hands.

"Meow?" Archie jumped up on the cushion next to me and head-butted my arm, demanding attention.

"It's just my imagination, right, boy?" I ignored the trembling in my hand as I obligingly ran it over his orange fur. "If there was anything outside, you'd know. Right?" His loud purr was all the response I needed.

I sat in silence and listened as the wind raged outside, eventually dozing off with Archie on my lap.

I awoke to the sun streaming through the living room window; the powerful wind of the night before had dissipated to a gentle breeze. Hurrying upstairs to use the bathroom, I took a quick shower and dressed in jeans and a white button-down shirt, slid my feet into my red converse sneakers and hurried back downstairs. Archie was waiting by the front door.

"Ready?" I asked, throwing the bolt and opening the door. He tore out ahead of me, found an appropriate spot in the garden and promptly dug a hole to pee in. Despite having a litter tray inside, Archie, I'd discovered, preferred to do his business outside among nature. Carrying my bag, phone, and keys I headed to my car. Unlocking the door, I turned to Archie. "Are you coming with me today, or staying?"

After he'd finished his morning toilet break and buried his hole he glanced my way, then turned his back, disappearing into the dunes with his tail in the air.

"Staying then!" I called after him, sliding behind the wheel of the car. Archie was the most independent cat I'd ever known. Some days he'd come with me to work at The Dusty Attic Bookstore, other days he'd stay home and sleep, and other days he'd take himself off exploring. One of his favorite places was the beach, and given he'd just headed off in the direction of our private track that led to the beach, I assumed that was his plan for today. That is, until I'd reversed the car and was just heading out when Archie appeared, carrying something in his mouth. Shoving the car into park, I rolled down my window.

"Whatcha got, boy?" I peered at what he held in his jaws, hoping it wasn't some poor little critter he'd found in the bushes. He mumbled a meow around the mouthful, then launched himself at my open window. With a squeal I pressed myself back against the seat to give him room to pass, hoping against hope that he didn't let go of the poor unfortunate critter in his mouth. Of course, that's exactly what he did. Sitting on the passenger seat, he set it down, then looked up at me expectantly. Reluctantly my eyes fell to...a leaf. My breath exhaled on a laugh. He'd brought me a leaf! Reaching over, I ruffled the fur on his head.

"Thanks, boy. That's wonderful."

"*Meow*," he responded, then lay down with his paws crossed, the leaf safely tucked beneath him in case it had any ideas of escape.

The drive into town took mere minutes and after parking behind my store I unlocked the door, fully prepared for Archie to burst ahead of me like he always did. Only this time was different. If the fact that Archie's fur stood on end and his tail was straight up in the air resembling a Christmas tree wasn't enough, the scent of sulfur in the air was a dead giveaway— something was up. Something of the demon variety.

"You smell it too, huh?" I muttered, edging around

him, putting my body between my familiar and whatever awaited us inside the bookstore.

Stepping over the threshold, I paused, eyes scanning the dim recesses of the store. While I couldn't see anything untoward, the hairs on the back of my neck stood on end warning me not to be complacent. Slowly I reached out a hand, felt along the wall for the light switch, and flicked it on.

"Oh, thank goodness you're here!" The ghost of Whitney Sims materialized in front of me and I couldn't contain a yelp of surprise.

"Whitney! What's going on? Can you smell that? Can ghosts even smell?" She was translucent enough that I could see through her but solid enough to block my view at the same time.

"Smell it?" She scoffed, nose raised. "I saw it!" She fanned a hand in front of her face dramatically.

"It?" I quizzed, leaning sideways to try and see around her.

She touched my arm, bringing my attention back to her with an icy blast. Leaning in close she whispered, "A goblin."

"A goblin?" I repeated in surprise. "Since when do goblins stink of sulfur?"

Her eyes narrowed. "Are you calling me a liar?"

"What? No!" Venturing further into the store, I sniffed. The smell was dissipating. "Where did it go?"

She blinked rapidly, and I caught the flash of guilt on her face but she wouldn't meet my eyes.

"What?" I demanded.

"What what?" she retaliated, arms crossed defensively across her chest as she hovered by my side.

"Where did it go, Whitney?"

"Harper Jones," she huffed, refusing to look at me. She drifted toward the front of the store and made a big deal about looking out the window. "I don't like your tone."

Rolling my eyes, I tried another tack. Whitney could be high strung on occasion.

"Sorry, Whitney," I lied. "I was a little taken aback, that's all. But it's wonderful news that you were here and saw the goblin, yeah? What can you tell me about it? Anything at all will help."

"Well," she began, turning to face me, "he was short. About this high." She held out a hand two feet off the ground. "And his skin was this grayish color. Old skin. Like leather. Thank the Lord he was wearing some sort of loincloth. Catching an eyeful of a goblin..." She trailed off, face screwed up in repulsion. "Gross. Anyway, he had a flat nose, yellow eyes—not a pretty yellow, not gold, just a dull yellow color. He had pointy ears and pointy teeth."

"How did he get in?"

"That's just it. He simply appeared—poof! Right in the middle of your store."

"And the smell? Was that his body odor do you think?"

She shook her head. "Oh no, that was his pee."

"His pee?!" What the hell? Whitney grinned and pointed toward a rapidly wilting potted plant in the reading corner.

"He peed on my plant?" To say I was shocked was an understatement. How rude.

"He did." She giggled, clearly finding the whole thing amusing.

Blowing out a breath, I approached the plant, the stench of sulfur increasing the closer I got. "Darn it, now we've got goblins to deal with too," I muttered, holding my hands out over the plant. I closed my eyes and chanted a healing spell. I'd never done one on a plant before and wasn't sure it would be effective, but thankfully the wilting and yellowing leaves returned to their glossy green sheen and the plant stood tall once more.

I had a thought. "Say, Whitney," I asked, crossing to the front door and propping it open to let some fresh air in, "you're a ghost. Jackson said the ghosts have been freaking out lately. What do you know about that? Have you heard anything?"

She didn't answer. "Whitney?" Spinning around, I scanned the store. She'd gone. That was weird. Whitney had died in my store and had decided this was her afterlife home. Initially, I only ever saw her when Jackson and I were together in the store, that somehow it was our powers combined that summoned her. Turned out that wasn't true at all, that Whitney wasn't tethered to me, the store, or Jackson, in any way whatsoever. With that new knowledge, Whitney would often pop in when it was just me. She liked to chat, to catch up on gossip and talk fashion, although I was of zero help in that department. For her to suddenly disappear—without saying goodbye—was another odd occurrence.

Pulling out my phone, I dialed Izzy. "Whitefall Cove now has goblins," I told her. "At least one. And I don't know if this is relevant, but apparently, it materialized directly in my store...is the Dusty Attic situated on a leyline by any chance?"

"Where's the goblin now?" Izzy asked.

I rolled my shoulders, trying to ease the tension pulling my muscles tight, "Not here. It peed on my potted plant and took off. FYI, goblin pee smells like sulfur...maybe we don't have a demon problem but a goblin problem?"

"Goblins are a breed of demon," she pointed out.

"Oh." Darn. I was hoping for an easy, less scary creature to have to deal with. Somehow a troublesome goblin didn't seem as bad as a demon.

"I'll pass that info on to Finn and Morgan. You raised a good question about Whitefall Cove and leylines, I'll ask them to look into it. And Llewellyn is arriving today. He'll take care of the goblin." Before I could respond, she'd hung up.

"Oh jeez, what's that smell?" Wendy, my assistant, stood in the open doorway, hand covering her nose.

"Yeah, it still stinks doesn't it?" I grimaced. "I'm going to have to call Gran and see if there's a spell to remove the sulfur stink. I hope it's not the same as skunk stink. I don't fancy a tomato juice bath."

THREE

Gran arrived, grimoire tucked under her arm. That wasn't what had me staring at her in surprise. No. What had me staring with my mouth hanging open was her outfit, or rather, her lack of anything remotely outrageous. Gran was known for her eccentric fashion choices. Bedazzled Ugg boots and clashing tutus were the norm for her. Not demure beige slacks, a white, buttoned up to the neck blouse, beige pumps, and a small white purse on a gold chain dangling from her elbow.

Wendy and I looked at each other.

"Gran?"

"Good morning, Harper, darling." She beamed, her makeup so understated I wasn't entirely sure she was wearing any, except for a slick of pale pink lipstick.

"Don't frown, darling." She tapped a finger against my forehead as she breezed past. "You'll get wrinkles."

"What's up with the outfit?"

Placing the grimoire on the counter next to the coffee pot, she glanced at me. "Why? What's wrong with it?"

"It's not your usual...look." I looked to Wendy again, who was clearly as surprised as I was, before turning my gaze back to Gran. "Is everything okay?"

Gran's eyes sharpened and narrowed, a flash of irritation gleaming in them before she turned her attention to the grimoire, flicking through the pages. "Let me see...." she muttered.

Wendy hurried over to my side where I was still glued to the spot, staring in disbelief.

"Something's up with your gran," she whispered.

"You think?" I snorted.

She elbowed me in the waist, hard. "No. Harper! Think about it. What did they say at the meeting last night? Report anything unusual, right?"

"You think I should report this?" I was more worried Gran may have had a stroke.

"I think she's possessed," Wendy hissed. "Look at her—your gran knows every spell in that book by heart. Why bring it here? And her clothes are a dead giveaway."

I felt the color drain from my face. How could I be

so stupid not to connect the dots and realize Wendy was right? Gran was possessed.

"Ooooh, this looks like a nice one." Demon-possessed Gran clapped her hands and, before I could stop her, read aloud the incantation in the book.

"Stop her!" Wendy hissed. "She could be about to turn us into toads!"

I was one second too late. With a poof, the store was suddenly full to bursting with roses.

"Oh my!" Gran declared. I couldn't see her anymore, thanks to the forest of flowers.

"Harper." Wendy sneezed. "Do something. My hay fever is going to kill me." She sneezed again.

"On it." Spitting a rose petal out of my mouth, I reversed the spell and as quickly as they'd arrived, the roses disappeared. Gran looked sheepish. Or whoever was possessing Gran looked sheepish.

I snatched up the grimoire before she could try anything else.

"It's okay, Gran, I'll take care of it." I shot a look at Wendy, mouthing to her to call Izzy. She nodded. Taking Gran's elbow, I led her toward the door. "Why don't you and I go get a nice hot cup of tea, hmmm?" I suggested, sliding the grimoire onto Wendy's desk as I passed.

"That would be lovely, Harper." She nodded in delight and hooked her arm through mine. I threw Wendy another look. Gran did not, ever, drink tea.

"We'll be across the road at Bean Me Up," I told Wendy. She nodded grim faced, phone already in hand.

We'd just stepped out the door when Gran squeezed my arm. "Would you look at that?" And pointed. Leaning forward, I peered around her.

Coming up the street was a beaten-up old RV, the body covered in roughly drawn sigils. As it drew level with the bookstore, the exhaust backfired with a loud bang and a cloud of smoke spat from beneath the vehicle.

I coughed, waving a hand in front of my face, catching a glimpse of the driver—a man in his mid to late twenties, dark hair, olive skin—before the ramshackle van rumbled past, straining as it towed a large trailer behind it. The trailer had a domed frame arching high from one side to the other. On the frame tied with twine, wire, and what appeared to be string, was a clear film of plastic, stretching across the frame. Beneath the plastic, dozens of plants, crammed onto shelves, hanging from the frame, pots of different sizes and colors filled the trailer. A mobile glasshouse. Despite its ramshackle appearance, it really was quite a brilliant idea.

My distraction with the van and trailer cost me. I turned to take Gran's arm and lead her across the street, only she was no longer by my side. Frantically glancing first one way, then the other, I could see no sign of her.

"Great," I muttered, hurrying across the road to Bean Me Up on the off chance she'd simply gone ahead of me. The bell above the door rang, announcing my presence and several heads turned my way with a chorus of greetings. But no Gran.

"Did any of you see where Gran went?" I asked.

Mrs. Helbety, who lived on the same street as Gran, responded. "I haven't seen her all day, love."

"Oh, but she was just out front a minute ago. I don't know where she could've gotten to."

"Are you sure? I didn't see her and I've been sitting by the window enjoying my Earl Grey for the past twenty minutes. Didn't see hide nor hair of her. Although I did clock the arrival of our demon hunter. Now he's a bit of all right, if I do say so myself." Mrs. Helbety was seventy if she was a day, and one hundred percent human.

"Gran isn't in her usual attire today," I admitted. "You may not have recognized her."

"Ooooh, gone incognito has she?" Mrs. Helbety cackled. "I'll bet she's gone out to the campgrounds to get an eyeful of Llewellyn Cox. He passed by just a minute ago. You must've seen him yourself, Harper."

"You mean the beaten-up old van towing the homemade trailer? That's our demon hunter?"

"You'll change your tune when you lay your eyes

on him, rest assured," Mrs. Helbety assured me, turning her attention back to her tea.

Thanking her, I stepped back onto the sidewalk and cast my eyes up and down once again. How could I have lost Gran? I knew she was quick on her feet, and if the demon possessing her thought I was on to him he'd have made for a hasty retreat. I was considering my options when my phone rang.

"Izzy," I answered.

"Wendy told me about your grandmother," she said without preamble. "Bring her to Drixworths. Finn is here and he thinks he can do an exorcism on his own."

"On his own? Isn't Morgan there?"

"She's gone to meet Llewellyn."

"Ahhh yeah, he just passed by here, complete with his own greenhouse."

Izzy chuckled. "Llewellyn is on the eccentric side, you could say. He's a gypsy on a heroic quest and as such he needs a supply of herbs close at hand for his potions."

"Potions? He's a witch then? A sorcerer?"

"You can ask him yourself when you meet him." Izzy cut me off. I could hear some sort of commotion in the background. "I've gotta go. Bring Gran."

"Wait!" I shouted before she disconnected the call. "That's the thing. She got away. Where would a demon possessing a witch go?"

"Your guess is as good as mine." And she hung up. My mouth dropped open at the abruptness, but then I figured Izzy had a lot on her plate and finding Gran wasn't her responsibility—it was mine. Crossing the road back to the Dusty Attic, I sniffed cautiously as I stepped over the threshold. The faint smell of sulfur still lingered.

"Back so soon?" Wendy asked, looking up from a consignment note clutched in her hand.

"Did Gran come back in here?" My eyes landed on the desk we used as a counter, the desk where I'd put Gran's grimoire. Only it wasn't there anymore.

"What? No, she didn't. Why?" Her eyes widened. "Did you lose her?"

My lips thinned into a straight line. After the godawful night I'd had, this was the last thing I needed. Not only had I lost Gran, but she was possessed. She'd be so pissed at me for this. Realizing Wendy was waiting for a response I grimly nodded.

"I don't suppose you moved the grimoire?" I was starting to put two and two together. The demon possessing Gran had taken advantage of my distraction when Llewellyn Cox had rolled into town and ducked back into the store and swiped the grimoire.

"I did." Wendy pulled out a drawer and lifted the grimoire out, smiling. "I figured I'd put it in here for safekeeping."

I hugged her. I'd never been so happy to be wrong. "You are a godsend. Thank you."

Wendy squeezed me before placing the grimoire back in the drawer and sliding it shut. As an extra measure, she turned the key and held it aloft. "I'll keep this safe and sound too. I figured the demon didn't really want the grimoire and is possibly not very familiar with spell casting because that spell it cast was woeful. Plus, if it was here for the grimoire then it wouldn't have brought it here, would it now?"

"You're right." Blowing out my breath, I closed my eyes for a second, gathering my thoughts. "I'm going to go look for her. You okay here?"

"Sure. You go, I'll be fine." She waved me away and once more I stepped outside onto the footpath. Where would a demon possessing a witch go?

After canvassing the Main Street, I headed to the Esplanade. So far no one had seen Gran, but then I feared they wouldn't have recognized her even if they had. I didn't even know Gran had such bland clothes in her wardrobe. Rounding the corner, I spied a woman in beige pants and a white blouse sitting out front of The Tea Leaf, Poppy and Hetty's tea shop.

"Gran?" Ugh, I shouldn't really call her that, but she turned her head and smiled at me as I hurried up the footpath towards her.

"Oh, hello again." She lifted a teacup, pinkie finger extended, and took a sip. "This peppermint tea is just delightful. You should try some, you look a little frazzled."

I blinked. Frazzled didn't begin to cover it. Poppy appeared, carrying a tray with two cups and saucers and a quaint teapot. She delivered it to the couple sitting a few tables over before eyeing me and cocking her head. I followed her inside.

"Is everything okay with your Gran?" she hissed in a stage whisper.

"Not really." Remembering Poppy's and Hetty's discomfort at the mention of demons at last night's meeting, I figured it was best they not know they had one sitting out front of their tea shop at this very second, apparently enjoying a cup of peppermint tea. "Has she been bothering you?"

Poppy shook her head. "Not at all. She's been most charming. Quite unlike Alice, I have to say."

I cleared my throat with a cough. "Must be that peppermint tea of yours." I watched Gran through the front window. "Looks like she's finished. How much do I owe you?"

"Oh, she already paid." Poppy patted my arm before disappearing behind the counter. Okay. One crisis averted. Now to get that demon out of Gran's body.

CHAPTER
FOUR

L lewellyn Cox was a sight to behold. Mrs. Helbety hadn't been wrong. As I'd approached his RV with Gran in tow, he'd flung open the door and stood framed in the doorway, shirtless, with worn denim jeans clinging low on his hips, corded thighs stretching the fabric tight.

"I knew you were coming." He grinned, his lilting Irish accent mesmerizing.

"You did?" I squeaked, then cleared my throat, eyes wide as he stepped down from his RV, bare feet silent on the ground as he stepped forward and into my personal space.

"How could I not?" he drawled, his intense green eyes surveying me from head to toe. His scent wrapped around me, vanilla and musk and something else so alluring I practically drooled.

"What are you doing?" I stumbled back, out of range of whatever spell he was using, my face troubled.

His grin flashed again, teeth white against the dark stubble covering the bottom half of his face. With his wild, shoulder-length hair and near nakedness and his scent—oh my God, his scent—he played havoc with my senses and had me forgetting the existence of my boyfriend. And just like that, the image of Jackson was akin to a bucket of cold water being dumped over my head.

"You're spell casting or doing something, I know that much," I grumbled. "Quit it. I'm not interested. I have a boyfriend."

He chuckled a low rumble from deep in his chest, making the white beads that dangled there jiggle with the movement.

"I assure you, I'm not doing anything. Whatever it is you're reacting to is all me."

"You smell funny," Gran announced, stepping close to him and sniffing before screwing up her face in apparent repulsion. I stared at her in shock.

Llewellyn's head whipped around and his eyes narrowed. "Ahhh." He nodded, taking a step back toward his RV but keeping his eyes on me.

"I see why you're here. Not just to welcome a weary traveler to your town."

"We all know why you're here." I frowned in

confusion. "You're a..." I hesitated. If whatever creature inhabiting Gran's body heard me say the words demon hunter, they'd bolt.

Llewellyn cut me off. "I had a vision. A vision where I'm to save the Whitelight Witch."

"The Whitelight Witch? Do you mean Morgan Healy?" I pictured the sorceress in my mind, with her dark skin and whiter than white hair.

Llewellyn snorted. "Hardly. She's a sorceress, not a witch, and she doesn't need saving. If anything, others need to be saved from her."

"What does that mean?"

"We'll talk after I've dealt with what you came for." Those intense green eyes of his moved from me to Gran. "Won't you come in for some tea?" he said to her.

"Oh tea?" She beamed. "I love tea. That would be lovely, thank you." Llewellyn stood back while Gran climbed the stairs and into the RV.

"You coming?" he asked.

Yes. I didn't want to miss this, but there was something about Llewellyn Cox that set my senses on edge, so it was with heavy feet that I made my way inside the RV. It was bigger than I'd expected. A huge bed dominated the rear, a colorful woven throw tossed over it, then a small kitchen area, some cupboards, and at the front of the vehicle two large chairs that spun to face either the front of the vehicle or rear.

"It's bigger than it looks." I couldn't help it, the words just slipped out. I closed my eyes for a second, hoping he wouldn't think it was some sort of come on.

"Happy to give you a tour," he drawled into my ear. Standing in the middle of the RV, he pointed at the bed. "Bedroom. Kitchen." Then he tapped a tall slim cupboard opposite the kitchen. "Closet. Next to that, the bathroom. And this here is the dining room." He touched the small square table situated behind the passenger seat.

"Cozy." I nodded, not knowing what else to say. I assumed it was a pretty standard layout for an RV but never having been in one before I had nothing to compare it too. Only Llewellyn's had something I'm betting no one else had. Herbs, crystals, dream catchers, candles. He had bric-a-brac everywhere. How he fit it all in I had no idea.

"Please, take a seat." He guided Gran to the passenger seat, swiveling it so it faced the table. Then he did the same for me, spinning the driver's seat and indicating I should sit. I did.

There wasn't enough room inside for us all to move about without touching, and despite his very attractive appearance, I did not want to be touching Llewellyn Cox. His raw sexuality and swaggering confidence told me he was used to getting his way with the ladies, and the lure of the king-sized bed mere feet away was too big to be ignored. He was a player, I was sure of it, and I had the sense Whitefall Cove was going to feel his presence in more ways than one.

"Relax," he said to me, busying himself in the kitchen, "I never go where I'm not wanted and you most definitely have a 'not interested' neon sign flashing above your head."

Heat filled my cheeks as I blushed. Was I that obvious? He chuckled and I wondered if he could read my mind.

"Would you just relax?" he muttered. "Your aura is suffocating me and I've got work to do. You are not in any danger from me, I can assure you."

Right, yes. Sucking in a deep breath, I willed myself to relax. We were here for Gran. We had to get this demon out of her and Llewellyn was the man for the job. Despite Izzy telling me to bring Gran to Finn and Morgan, I'd felt drawn to bring her here, to this man.

"You'd do good to follow your instincts," he said, filling an electric kettle with water and setting it to boil. "I see you're an over-thinker—not good for stress." Pulling out a mug, he set it on the sink, then ran his fingers along a row of jars, finally tapping one and lifting it down, spooning the contents into the mug.

The kettle boiled and he poured the steaming water into the mug, stirred, then handed it to Gran. At the precise moment her hand wrapped around the mug and her fingers touched his, he spoke, "Spirits of air, forest, and sea, set us of this demon free; beasts of hoof and beasts of shell, drive this evil back to Hell."

A blast of black smoke streaked out of Gran and I let out a startled scream, pressing back in my seat. Llewellyn held firm, his fingers wrapped over Gran's on the mug as the cloud of black smoke whirled around the room before slithering under the door, leaving an odd void of sensation in its wake.

"Finally," Gran muttered, snatching her hand away from the mug. "I don't drink tea. What were you thinking? And what in all that's holy am I wearing?"

"Oh, thank God!" Reaching over, I clasped Gran's hand. "You're back."

"How are you feeling?" Llewellyn took a sip of the tea and studied Gran over the rim of the cup.

"Wait." I frowned. "What's in that tea?"

"This?" He held up the mug. "Chamomile. You should try it, very relaxing. You are way too wound up."

"Not surprising considering my Gran was possessed by a demon," I grumbled, feeling attacked.

"Yes, well, if you two don't mind." Gran got to her feet, holding her arms out from her body as if she'd been dunked into something unpleasant, "I'd like to go shower and scrub that...whatever it was...off me. Not to mention burn these clothes!" Heading toward the door, she stopped suddenly when she reached Llewellyn.

"Thank you," she said. And kissed him. Not a matronly peck on the cheek either. A full kiss on the lips that went on for several seconds. Llewellyn, to his credit, didn't pull away. Breaking the kiss, Gran stroked his bare chest with one hand, slapped his denim-covered rear with the other, winked, and was gone. I blinked, not believing what I'd just witnessed.

"Don't apologize," Llewellyn growled.

I blinked again. "I wasn't going to!"

"You were. You could afford to take a page out of your grandmother's book and loosen up a little. She was thankful for what I'd done and expressed herself appropriately."

"What? You're suggesting I kiss you too? To say thanks?" I snorted, rising to my feet. "Not going to happen."

Llewellyn's grin disappeared, replaced by a frown. "That's not how I do business and you know it." His tone told me I'd offended him, and replaying the words I'd just said in my mind, I realized he was right. That was rude of me. Something about him set me on edge and I'd lashed out. I guess Gran wasn't the only one acting out of character today.

"I'm sorry," I admitted. "That was rude. How much do I owe you?"

Llewellyn, it appeared, was quick to forgive, for that grin was back. "The first one's on the house."

I'd had my hand in my purse but paused. "You're sure?"

"I'll do you a deal."

I opened my mouth to shut him down, but his grin widened, revealing even white teeth. "Not that type of deal. Boy, you have a dirty mind. And I know that's what you were thinking by the pink in your cheeks."

The pink in my cheeks must surely be fire engine red by now and I resisted the urge to fan myself.

"No, but seriously..." His voice sobered and he waved to the seat behind me. "Please sit for a minute. I'd like to talk to you."

"About the Whitelight Witch?"

He eased himself into the seat Gran had vacated and sipped his chamomile tea. "Sure."

Resuming my seat, I watched him. "I've never heard of her before."

"She's a witch with the power of advanced telekinesis. Very powerful."

"Advanced telekinesis?"

"So basic telekinesis is where you can move objects with your mind, yes?"

I nodded in understanding and he continued, "Advanced telekinesis is where you can move more than one object at once, or move them far, far, away. Plus they can access telekinetic energy. But what is important here is that she's in danger. She needs protection."

I looked at him helplessly. "Honestly, I have no idea what you're talking about. Are you sure it wasn't Morgan you saw in your vision? She has white hair."

He shook his head. "I'm sure. It's not Morgan."

"What did you mean earlier? When you said people needed protecting from her?"

"Morgan's a descendant of the Queen of Avalon." Another sip of tea.

"So?" I had no idea who the Queen of Avalon was.

"So she uses her supernatural gifts to bewitch and manipulate humans for her own ends."

My eyes widened. "Are you serious?" Why would Izzy have invited a sorceress to help us if it meant said sorceress was a danger to us?

"Desperate times call for desperate measures." Llewellyn studied his tea, face intent.

"Can you read my mind?" I demanded.

He chuckled. "Nope. But"—he looked up and his green eyes dazzled me, seemingly to glow—"I think I am here for you."

I couldn't look away, the green eyes probing, burning into my mind.

"What?" My voice came out three octaves higher than usual and I cleared my throat.

"You..." He leaned toward me and placed his hand on my arm. It burned. "Are not using your powers to your full potential. You are denying your power. You have pushed your magic into a prison of your own making. I can break it free."

I reared back, breaking contact with him, rubbing my hand over my arm where his touch had burned like acid. Who was he? What was he?

"Sorry. That came out a little intense, huh?" He grinned again and took another sip of his tea. "I can feel this power within you—kinda like a vibration. But you're fighting it. I can help. Magic is nothing to be afraid of."

"Everyone has been telling me I'm a powerful witch," I admitted, turning my gaze to the window and the trailer park outside. It all looked so innocent, so mundane, yet here in this RV, he was saying words that caused my heart to beat frantically in my chest.

"I'm wondering if you are the Whitelight Witch." He spoke so softly I barely heard.

I was already shaking my head. "Sorry, not me. I have no telekinetic ability whatsoever."

Feeling the urge to flee, I stood, looking down at him. "Thanks for helping Gran," I said, not knowing what else to say.

"You're welcome. One last thing, Harper." I blinked in surprise. How did he know my name? I'd never introduced myself. "Don't trust Morgan. Or Finn. He may be a druid, but he's from the Otherworld." He said it as if the Otherworld were not to be trusted, a dimension where evil is spawned. I'd never considered it one way or another, but now that he'd planted that little seed I couldn't help but wonder...was he right?

"I don't believe Izzy would have asked them here to help us if they couldn't be trusted," I argued.

"They hide behind a web of lies and illusion," was his cryptic response. Then said abruptly, "Until we meet again."

Suitably dismissed I opened the door and climbed down from the RV and had taken several steps when I heard him call out behind me. "I meant what I said. I can help you with your magic. Think about it, Harper."

I hurried away, more rattled than I cared to admit. And then I remembered I hadn't told him about the goblin but wasn't brave enough to turn back and ask. Damn it.

CHAPTER
FIVE

Three goblin heads swiveled in my direction, faces a combination of surprise and guilt, before they each took off in different directions, leaving behind a stench that burned my eyes. Gagging, I pressed my nose and mouth into the crook of my elbow and ventured further inside my bookstore. Seemed like the stinky little vermin were multiplying.

Wendy had closed up for lunch and I'd just returned from the demon-vanquishing session with Gran and Llewellyn, not expecting to find even more goblins, let alone in my store. With sulfur thick in the air and a sizzling sound echoing and bouncing off the walls, I cautiously began the search. "Serves me right for not going back and asking Llewellyn about goblins," I muttered to myself, eyes watering. Gah, had they peed everywhere? Waving my hand behind me, I sent a dash of magic to prop open the front door. These guys were worse than skunks!

Not only stinkier. But faster. I'd just catch a peep of one poking its ugly face around a bookcase and before I could blink he was gone. Around and around the store I chased them, stopping to repair the damage from their toxic pee where they'd taken a whizz against a chair or a bookshelf. I vaguely wondered if goblins had bladder issues because this was a serious amount of pee. Like...serious.

"Oh, for the love of pancakes!" Gran announced. "Child, this place reeks!"

"I know, you don't need to tell me twice." My voice was muffled by my sleeve. I glanced over at her where she stood in the doorway, relieved beyond measure at the sight of her in black and white striped leg warmers, a skin-tight thigh-high dress with a pentacle design glimmering in silver across the chest. And of course, bright orange bedazzled Ugg boots. I wanted to hug her, but I didn't want to lower my arm from my face just in case all this goblin pee melted my skin.

"You got yourself a goblin infestation," she said, hands on hips as her eyes tracked the progress of the goblins zipping around the store.

"Thank you, Captain Obvious." I coughed, blinking my stinging eyes.

"Ooooh, sass. I like it." She grinned, sauntered into

the store as if the paint wasn't peeling from the walls with the stench. "Why is my grimoire here?" She paused mid-stride and shot me a sharp glare.

Knowing she could sense her book of magic recipes but not having time to go into an explanation —not while the goblins were destroying my store—I threw out an offhand. "Safe-keeping. I'll explain later —after we've dealt with the goblins. Do you know how to get rid of them?"

"Pft. Easy peasy." Pulling her wand from her cleavage, she waved it in the air and singsonged, "Bud-a-bing-bud-a-boom!" With a pop, all three goblins disappeared.

"Seriously? Bud-a-bing-bud-a-boom?"

She laughed, shaking her head. "Of course not. That's just for dramatic flair."

"You've got plenty of dramatic flair without adding more. That took care of the goblins, but what about all this damage?" My heart hurt at the destroyed books that had melted like ice on a hot day thanks to the goblin's toxic urine. Why, oh why did they feel the need to pee on everything?

"You can do this yourself, you know," Gran grumbled, but dutifully waved her wand and order was restored to the bookstore—along with clean, fresh, air. I lowered my arm and dragged in a lungful.

"Why do they keep appearing here?" I wondered out loud, not expecting Gran to have an answer. And hoping to distract her from the discussion about my magic. Llewellyn had been right, as much as it irked me to admit it. I wasn't using my magic to my full ability. In fact, I was sliding back into old habits.

When I'd moved from Whitefall Cove to the city I'd decided to live my life as a human and ignore the witch within. All was fine until the day I caught my fiancée cheating on me and my magic surged forth—costing me my witch's license on top of other things, such as my job and relationship. It wasn't until I returned to my hometown of Whitefall Cove and attended Drixworths Academy for a refresher course and to re-sit my witches exam that I realized how much I'd missed using my powers.

And yet here I was, not using them, or not knowing how to use them to full effect. After completing my refresher course at Drixworths, everyone had been telling me what a powerful witch I was, how I didn't need a wand to channel my magic. In fact, they'd assigned me Archie, my orange cat, as a familiar to help me keep control of my magic. It was that powerful. Apparently. Which reminded me.

"Have you ever heard of the Whitelight Witch?" I asked Gran.

She'd placed her hand on top of the desk where her grimoire was locked away and with a click, the drawer slid open and the book levitated to her outstretched hands. "Hmmm? Whitelight Witch? Nope, can't say I have." Tucking the grimoire under her arm, she gave it a loving pat. "Why?"

I shook my head. "Nothing. Just something Llewellyn said."

"Oh? He's hot, isn't he?" Gran's face took on a dreamlike quality while she fantasized about the demon hunter currently residing in our trailer park.

"I have a boyfriend!" I protested, ignoring the little voice inside my head that assured me Llewellyn Cox, demon hunter, was most certainly hot.

"Pft, not for you!" Gran cackled. "For me!"

A laugh snort burst forth. Of course, I should have realized. Gran had an appetite for younger men. Hell, any man really.

"Well, you did kiss him," I pointed out and she touched her fingers to her bottom lip. "I did, didn't I? Now that I'm all cleaned up and back in my own skin, I might just pay him a little visit. To say thank you, you know?"

"Gran," I warned, "you already did. Plus I'm sure he's got work to do. I don't think you should be disturbing him."

Of course, she ignored me, sweeping out of the store and calling back over her shoulder, "You should ward your store, you know, to keep those goblins out." And then she was gone.

"Ward the store," I muttered under my breath. So damn obvious, but it had totally slipped past me. But when we'd warded my cottage, my entire coven was involved. I didn't have six witches at my disposal today. There was just me. Would a ward even hold? But I figured it couldn't hurt, I had to at least try.

"Mreooow?"

"Oh hey, Archie!" I bent and scooped my furry familiar into my arms, dropping a kiss on his head. "Where did you get to, boy? Those goblins scare you, huh?"

"Mrrrrt," he protested, flexing his claws on my shoulder.

"No?" I chuckled, running my hand over his fur. "Okay then. So I need to ward this place—only I don't have the coven with me and it's a bit risky doing it during opening hours. Should I wait until tonight? Get the coven here and do it properly?"

Archie hissed, which took me by surprise. He rarely hissed. He talked to me in meows and odd little mrrrt noises, not hisses and growls.

"You're saying I should do it now?" Placing him on the desk I stood with my hands on my hips while I tried to remember what I'd need. Annie, the head witch of the Sisters of the Sacred Flame Coven had taken care of all the details when we warded my home —this time it was down to me. Pulling out my phone, I dialed Wendy's number.

"Before you come back, do you think you could

pick up some supplies for me?" I asked when she answered.

"Of course. What do you need?"

"I need to ward the store. We have a goblin problem."

"The goblin came back?"

"With friends."

"Leave it with me. Is your coven coming?"

I shook my head. "No, I'm going to have a go myself and if it doesn't work I'll get their help tonight. I just need it to hold for the afternoon."

"Oh...well...I know I don't belong to a coven, and my magic is a little rusty, but I'd be happy to help," Wendy offered.

"Yes! I'll take any help I can get. Archie is here. He can help channel my magic, and with you as well that may be just enough juice to get the job done. You know what we need, right?" I was hoping she did because I wasn't sure I remembered all the details correctly.

"Sure. I'll grab some sage as well so we can smudge first. Won't be long." She hung up before I could respond, but true to her word, it must've only been five minutes before she bustled through the door, heaving a shopping bag onto the desk.

"All here." She puffed, turning back to lock the front door, flipping the open sign to closed.

Digging through the bag, I pulled out the bundle of

sage, lit it with a flick of my fingers, then extinguished the flame, leaving only smoke.

"You remember what to do?" I asked Wendy. She nodded. "I smudge all the time. Don't you?"

I bit my lip, considered lying, then admitted, "Not really? Things have been sliding a bit...magic wise."

She blinked at me. Then cleared her throat. "Oh. Okay, well...use your hand to waft the smoke over your body from your feet up to your head and back down to your feet. At the same time chant 'air, fire, water, earth, cleanse, dismiss, dispel.'"

I nodded and did as instructed. Once I'd smudged myself I handed the sage to Wendy who repeated the process, then hurried around the store, waving the smoke into every nook and cranny before returning and leaving the sage burning in an empty coffee cup.

"Do you remember how to ward?" she asked, digging around in the shopping bag.

"Now that I do remember!" I declared. "I regularly strengthen the wards at home."

"Strengthening isn't the same as establishing," Wendy pointed out, "but between us, we'll muddle through."

"I guess I'll start with air," I said, holding up a feather.

Wendy tipped some sand from a tiny zip-locked bag into her palm. "I'll be earth."

I walked the perimeter of the store chanting, "By

air, I ward thee. Guard this space from all ill will and all those who wish us harm." Wendy did the same, chanting earth instead of air, then we both returned to the desk.

"I'll do fire," Wendy said, picking up a candle and lighting it.

"That leaves water." I opened the other ziplock bag and an ice cube tumbled into my hand. Together we repeated the chant, pacing around the store before meeting back at the desk.

"All done." Wendy blew out the candle and set it on the desk.

My ice cube had melted and I wiped my wet hands on the legs of my jeans. "Not quite. At the cottage, I had to strengthen the ward with my magic."

Wendy's eyes widened and her mouth formed a little Oh.

"What?" I asked, wondering why she looked surprised.

"Oh nothing." She scratched her head. "I'd just never heard that that was necessary. But yeah, okay, do your thing. I'll clear this stuff away and we'll be open for business."

Closing my eyes, I visualized the ward, of pouring my energy into it. When I'd done this at my cottage I'd felt it like a physical manifestation, but this time? Nothing. I frowned. Maybe it was because Wendy wasn't a member of my coven; therefore her magic didn't bind as tightly to mine.

"I'll move the sage to the storeroom," Wendy said. "Don't need to alert the customers that we're having issues."

I opened my eyes in time to see her retreating back and smoke wafting around her. With a shrug, I flipped the closed sign to open. Time to sell some books.

CHAPTER

SIX

"I'm worried," I admitted to Jackson over dinner that evening at Brewed Awakening.

Monica, my vampire best friend, worked behind the bar and due to our different daylight schedules, I tried to drop in a few times a week to catch up. Tonight was one of those times. Only Monica was busy. A busload of tourists were in town and were currently enjoying her cocktail-making skills. Thank goodness she was a vampire and could move super fast—just as quickly as someone ordered a drink, it was placed in front of them with a fang-revealing grin. The tourists loved it.

"Why's that?" Jackson ran his thumb over the back of my hand and I turned my attention back to him.

"With what's happening in Whitefall Cove. The wards. The demons. Finn and Morgan. All of it." I'd been unsettled ever since Izzy had called the town meeting.

"Don't forget Llewellyn Cox," Jackson drawled, a twinkle in his eye.

I snorted. "Who could forget him? I didn't think the presence of a druid and a sorceress could be upstaged, but I think a particular Irish demon hunter has managed it."

"At least with the ladies." Jackson grinned. I'd told him about my encounter with Llewellyn, and of his offer to help with my magic. I still didn't know what to think of the whole situation.

"Not this one," I grumbled. Sure, Llewellyn was an attractive guy, and he had a magnetism that drew you in, but there was something about him that I just couldn't put my finger on. I wasn't one hundred percent convinced I could trust him. And all the nonsense he'd sprouted about the Whitelight Witch, another worry to add to the mountain of worries whirling through my brain.

"Babe." Jackson interlaced his fingers with mine and grinned, the adorable dimple in his cheek flashing. "You don't have to convince me. I know how you feel about me...and I'm not the jealous type."

I cocked a brow. "No?" Certain memories of bad boy lawyer Blake Tennant flashed before my eyes. Jackson had definitely been jealous then.

He was shaking his head when something caught

his attention over my shoulder. His face went slack and his fingers loosened their grip on mine. What had he seen?

"Jackson?" Swiveling my head, I looked behind me. Nothing. Well, nothing but the crowd of tourists milling about, making a godawful racket as the effects of Monica's cocktails kicked in.

Jackson's hand fell with a thunk to the table and when I glanced back at him his face was a ghastly grey color.

"What's wrong?" I whispered, the hairs on the back of my neck standing on end. But he ignored me. Or didn't hear me. I suspected it was the latter because Jackson looked like he'd seen a ghost—which wasn't unusual for a necromancer, but this was different. He looked totally freaked out.

"Bryan," he choked, stumbling to his feet, his chair tipping over behind him.

"Who?" I looked around again, trying to see what he was seeing. Nope, I had nothing.

Jackson bolted for the door, taking me by surprise. "Wait here! I'll be back."

"Jackson!" I called, following behind, but the crowd was thick and as I wriggled my way between the patrons I lost sight of him. At the door, I collided with none other than Llewellyn Cox. And Gran.

"Slow down there." Llewellyn steadied me with a hand on my shoulder, which I instantly shrugged off. I leaned to the left, trying to see around him, but he blocked my view. Annoyed and frustrated, I turned to Gran, only to stop cold.

"What. Are. You. Wearing?" I choked.

She looked down at herself and then back at me. "A bikini!" Her smile was dazzling...as was the cat eye makeup winging up the side of her face in neon blue. The bikini itself was a crochet number. Stripes. In a rainbow of colors. I swallowed, risked a glance at her feet, felt my lips twitch. Yep, bedazzled Ugg boots, also in a rainbow of colors.

Clearing my throat, I asked, "Aren't you cold?"

"Not with this hunk-oh-spunk keeping me warm." It was then I noticed their linked arms.

"Are you two on a date?" The notion wasn't absurd. Not with Gran.

"Would it matter if we were?" Llewellyn was looking over my head to the room beyond. I clocked the exact moment his eyes landed on Monica, the slight widening and then narrowing as he tracked her movements along the bar.

"Not to me. But if you hurt Gran..." I trailed off, my warning clear.

"Relax, White One, she's buying me a drink to say thank you for booting her unwanted tenant."

"White One?" Gran cackled. "Her tan ain't that bad, Irish." Then Gran tugged him forward, and after some slight bumping and maneuvering, we'd navigated past each other and I had access to the door.

Rushing outside, I stood for a moment, the night air cool against my skin, the sudden lack of noise startling, my ears ringing from the chaotic sounds inside Brewed Awakening.

"Jackson?" I yelled. I'd expected him to be waiting outside, maybe catching some fresh air. But he wasn't here. He'd disappeared. Jogging down the darkened street, I kept my eyes peeled. Where had he gone? I slowed to a stop, breathing heavily. The night was still and silent and I strained my ears, listening for footsteps.

"Of course, you idiot..." Muttering to myself I retraced my steps. We'd driven here in Jackson's car. If his car was still here, then he couldn't be far.

Only his car was gone. I felt like such an idiot for not noticing earlier.

Pulling out my phone, I dialed his number, but he didn't pick up. Instead, I left him a voice mail. "Jackson? Umm...is everything okay? You kinda left me stranded here?" I paused, remembering how freaked out he'd looked. "But don't worry about it. I'll find my own way home. I just want to make sure you're okay? Call me. Please."

Hanging up, I turned to go back inside Brewed Awakening, figuring I'd get Gran to give me a lift home, or hang around until closing and catch a lift with Monica, but looking through the window I reconsidered my options. I wasn't in the mood. Gran was flirting up a storm with Llewellyn, who was shamelessly indulging her. Monica was super busy at the bar, and considering the place was jam-packed, I'd bet it would be a late night for her. And me, if I hung about.

I had a sudden yearning for my pj's, a glass of wine, and the solitude of my cottage on the bluff. Deciding it was a nice night for a walk, I headed off, noticing as I did so that each lamp post I passed the light flickered off. At the end of the street, I looked back, a shiver dancing over my skin at the darkness looming over Main Street with all the streetlights out. I hurried down a side road towards the Esplanade, which, when I reached it, was fully lit.

Slowing my breathing, I tried to calm my racing mind. Stop imaging the worst, I scolded myself.

Stopping out front of The Twinkle Star, a women's fashion store, I pulled out my phone, deciding to call an Uber rather than continue to scare myself silly with my overactive imagination. Only my phone was dead. "What the hell?" I tried turning it off, then on again, but the screen remained black.

When I glanced up, I froze. In the reflection of The Twinkle Star's window was...something. A woman? She appeared to be floating. Frowning, I spun, only nothing was there. I looked back at the window, but the reflection I thought I'd seen had disappeared.

"I think I'm losing my mind." A scurrying noise and the rattle of rubbish cans came from the alley to my right. Something was seriously off with this whole evening and I berated myself for thinking it was a smart idea to walk home, alone, in the dark, when I knew we had a demon problem.

"What is wrong with you, Harper Jones?" Of course, the question was rhetorical. I wasn't expecting an answer, so when I got one, I screamed out loud.

"Sorry." Llewellyn Cox sat astride a scooter, one foot on the curb, the engine rumbling. "Didn't mean to startle you. Thought you would have heard me approach."

Hand to my thundering heart, I looked up and down the street. How had I not heard him? And where did he get a scooter?

"Keep this little beauty anchored to the back of my RV—makes getting around when I'm camped a whole lot easier." Again, it was as if he was reading my mind.

"What are you doing here? Aren't you on a date with my Gran?"

He blinked at me, remained silent for a moment, then said. "I dropped her home about an hour ago."

"An hour ago? That's not possible, I literally ran into the two of you at Brewed Awakening no more than ten minutes ago!"

"Harper, that was hours ago."

Anger bubbled through me. I didn't know what game he was playing, but I didn't appreciate him messing with me. Crossing my arms over my chest and planting my feet, I said, "Bullshit."

Pulling out his phone, he hit the screen, then held it out so I could read it. 2:00 a.m. glowed starkly on the phone.

"You're trying to trick me. You could have set that to read whatever time you like. It's not two in the morning, more like eight in the evening."

He shook his head and sighed. "Whatever. I'm not going to argue with you. I have better things to do than change the time on my phone just to play some trick on you. Now, do you want a lift or not?"

"A lift?"

He rolled his shoulders, looked away and then back at me, brows drawn low. "You looked freaked out when I pulled up. I asked if you wanted a lift."

"You did?" Why didn't I remember that? Or was he lying? My head started to ache and I rubbed a weary hand around the back of my neck, realizing how very tired I was. Was he right? Had I been wandering the streets of Whitefall Cove for over six hours?

"Hop on. I'll drop you home." It was no longer an invitation, but an order, and rather than get affronted I meekly complied. I was tired and he was offering a lifeline. Throwing one leg over the seat behind him, I tried to keep some distance between us, but it was impossible. My legs immediately cradled the back of his thighs and I could feel a rush of heat burn my face.

"Hold on." He gunned the engine, but rather than reach my arms around his waist, I reached behind me and clung to the back of the seat instead. I'm pretty sure I heard him chuckle. I was fully expecting him to roar away from the curb at breakneck speeds, so color me surprised when he slowly putted away, his maximum speed slightly faster than what I could jog.

"Doesn't this thing go any faster?"

"Daisy here does her best work at a slower pace," he replied. "Okay, White, you're going to have to give me some directions here. Where do you live?"

"Oh, right. I live in the lighthouse caretaker's cottage, up on the bluff." I was brave enough to release one hand from its death grip on the back of the seat to point toward the bluff.

"Oh cool, the lighthouse is on my list of places to see." With a nod, he headed in the general direction of the bluff. There was only one road in and out to the lighthouse so it wasn't incredibly difficult to find and I slowly relaxed—just a fraction—as we puttered our way towards it.

Once we'd arrived, he didn't kill the engine, just left it idling while I awkwardly dismounted and thanked him for the lift.

"Any time, White." He nodded, getting ready to leave.

I stopped him. "If it really is two in the morning, what are you doing driving around? Why aren't you home in bed?"

"I was about to visit a friend. Which I still intend to do. But now I'm late, so if you'll excuse me." And off he went, with a *put-put-put* that made me smile despite myself.

"I don't know what game you're playing with me, Llewellyn Cox, but I'm on to you." Of course, he couldn't hear me, but I was quietly confident in my assessment. He was lying and was just pulling my chain, playing some sort of joke at my expense. So of course when I stepped inside the cottage and my eyes landed on the clock I was freaked out all over again. The time read two fifteen. He hadn't been lying. But how the hell did I lose track of all that time?

CHAPTER
SEVEN

I didn't think I'd be able to sleep, but the minute my head hit the pillow I was out. But my sleep wasn't restful. I tossed and turned all night, hovering on the edge of wakefulness and slumber, so when my eyes popped open at seven thirty I was up and out of bed immediately, glad to leave the night behind. My dreams had been torturous affairs, so much so, Archie had abandoned his position curled up by my side and was currently nowhere to be seen. I assumed he'd decamped to the sofa or found himself some other comfy spot that didn't involve being continually disturbed. Stumbling into the bathroom, I took a hot shower which revived me enough that I felt human. Sort of, if you factored in the fact that I'm a witch. Llewellyn's words echoed in my head, niggling away. I should pay more attention to my powers; I should show more interest in all things witch related. Coulda, shoulda, woulda.

A dusting of makeup to hide the shadows under my eyes, and I hurried downstairs, picked up my phone where I'd left it charging on the dresser by the stairs, and immediately dialed Jackson's number.

"You've reached Detective Ward. Leave a message." *Beep*.

I left Jackson another message, hoping I'd disguised the worry in my voice. He'd seen something last night, something that had him bolting out of Brewed Awakening without a second thought. Or, more precisely, thought for me. I didn't want to dwell on how much that hurt. Something bigger was at play in Whitefall Cove and I couldn't afford the luxury of hurt feelings to get in the way of discovering exactly what was going on. And how to stop it.

Thankfully, it looked like time had restored itself unless I'd been asleep longer than I'd realized, but the clock in the kitchen read seven forty-five and the early morning light streaming through the windows assured me it was daybreak and not sunset.

"Meow." Right on cue, Archie appeared, rubbing around my ankles as I prepared the coffee. Mornings like this demanded caffeine and I suspected I'd be hitting this particular beverage hard just to get through the day. After refilling Archie's kibble, I crossed to the front door to let him out for his morning

toilet break. I stood on the threshold, hesitant to step foot outside. Everything had been so wonky lately and last night had rattled me. The one place I felt safe, the one place I was confident could not be breached, was my cottage. Stepping foot outside meant I was vulnerable again. I didn't know what entity had been playing with me last night, but I was certain it was something supernatural. But it hadn't possessed me...at least I don't think it had, but then again, I mused, I had lost hours of time so maybe I had been possessed and that would account for it. But then...why did the demon leave? Or did Llewellyn perform an exorcism and I just didn't know it? Urgh, just the thought of it made me want to shower again.

The twinge of pain in my temple was back, warning me I was overthinking things. Again. Leaving the front door ajar for Archie, I dialed Gran.

"Is your house on fire?" she answered, voice as rough as sandpaper.

"What?" I blinked, surprised. "No...should it be?"

"That's the only explanation I will accept for you calling me at this ungodly hour," she grumbled. I heard the rustle of covers, a grunt, a fart, and smiled. Of course, she was still in bed.

"Late night?" I teased, pretending I didn't know that Llewellyn had dropped her home after midnight.

"Early morning. Make it quick. Now you've woken me I've got to pee."

"Can we ward ourselves against demon possession?" I blurted.

"Not ward per se, but there are talismans we can wear that would repel demon possession." The bed creaked and I visualized her sitting on the edge, wedging her feet into her furry slippers.

"So why aren't we doing that? Why didn't Izzy even suggest that at the town meeting? I mean it seems like a pretty standard measure of protection." One that I'd only just thought of, but glossing over that little fact, I continued. "And warding our homes and businesses."

"I think Izzy has enough on her plate with Finn and Morgan." Another fart as she stood and then shuffling across the floor. "They should have gotten the wards repaired by now so the personal steps you mention wouldn't have been necessary."

"So...." I jumped on what she'd just said. "You're saying the wards aren't repaired?"

"Well, if the goblin playing in my front garden when I got home this morning is any indication, no." Then I heard it. The tickling sound of water.

"Gran...are you in the bathroom? Peeing?"

"I'm about to poop," she confirmed.

I hung up without saying goodbye.

"I think it's time we got to the bottom of what's really going on," I said to Archie, who'd eaten a sturdy breakfast of two kibble biscuits and was now approaching the front door I'd opened earlier. I'd been reluctant to cross the threshold, but there was no way I'd let Archie out there alone, so pushing down my misgivings, I followed my ginger ball of fluff and stood guard while he dug his little hole.

"Good morning, Harper!"

My head snapped up and I squinted into the sun, eventually spotting Poppy and Hetty Oliver power walking in matching pale blue velour sweatpants, arms pumping as their hips snapped from side to side.

"Hetty. Poppy." I nodded in greeting. Archie was still occupied with bathroom duties so I crossed to the white picket fence separating my front garden from the walking trail to the lighthouse and waited while they approached. "Nice morning for it." And it was. A dusting of white fluffy clouds decorated the sky, a slight breeze ruffled my hair, birds were chirping and I could hear the hum of bees where they visited the lavender bush near my front gate. You wouldn't know we were in the grip of a demon invasion.

They drew to a stop, looked at each other and then at me.

"This ward business is concerning," Hetty said, glancing around as if concerned she'd be overheard. Considering I was the only one who lived out here she had absolutely nothing to worry about.

"It is," I agreed. "Although with the help we have on hand, I'm sure it will be settled in no time." I did my best to sound positive, despite having my doubts that Finn and Morgan were up to the task.

Poppy tskd. "A druid and a sorceress. And still, the wards aren't fixed."

"Have you had any trouble?"

"We think we have a poltergeist in the shop!" Hetty blurted, then flinched when Poppy slapped her arm to shush her.

"A poltergeist?" I was impressed. All I'd had were peeing goblins. And whatever had decided to mess with me last night. "You should go see Llewellyn about that."

"The demon hunter?" Hetty positively swooned. "We saw him arrive yesterday...so dreamy." She fanned her face dramatically.

Poppy sighed and crossed her arms over her chest. "Yes, well, looks aside"—she frowned sternly at her sister—"we were intending to drop by to visit him anyway."

"Oh?" It was more polite conversation than a burning desire to know why the Oliver sisters wanted to see a certain Irish demon hunter.

"His glasshouse is incredibly well-stocked." Poppy nodded.

"He's well-stocked," Hetty muttered, then blushed.

Poppy shook her head at her sister. "We need to restock some of our herbs."

"For the tea shop," Hetty cut in.

Poppy nodded. "For the tea shop."

"Well yes, good idea. I'm sure he has a good selection." I had no idea if he did nor not.

"How about you?" Poppy asked, narrowing her eyes and leaning in a little too close for comfort.

"Me?" I leaned away.

"Any trouble?" she pressed.

"Oh. Yes." I nodded. "Goblins, of all things. Did you know they pee sulfur?"

Both Poppy and Hetty blinked at me, faces blank, before they glanced at each other and both said at once, "Isn't that interesting?"

Okay, the Oliver sisters were seriously weird. I swear I didn't say it out loud but both of them stiffened, side-eyed each other, then said, "We'll be on our way. Have a good day." And off they went, power walking up the trail. I watched until they rounded a bend.

"That was weird," I said to Archie, who now sat rubbing his face against my calf. Scooping him up, I buried my face in his fur. "They were weird."

"Meow," he replied.

"Anyway, time to get a move on." Keeping him clutched to my chest, I headed back inside. No sign of paranormal activity this morning, but I didn't want to linger. "First up we're going to see Izzy. I get the feeling there's more to this than she's letting on. Plus I want to know if these so-called experts that she's called in have any talismans."

"Mrrrrrt."

"I think so too." I nodded, kicking the front door closed with my foot, scooping up my bag and keys and heading out the back door, still with Archie clutched to my chest. "Is there anything I'm missing?" I asked him.

"Mreooow, mrt, mrt, mraaaaawh," he replied, head bumping my chin.

"I'm sure we could get a talisman for your collar," I assured him. Opening the car door, I waited for Archie to scoot over to the passenger seat before sliding behind the wheel. Hooking my phone up to the vehicle's Bluetooth, I called Wendy. "Are you okay to open and manage the store on your own this morning?" I asked when she picked up.

"Of course."

"I could send Gran in to help," I offered. At least I knew she was awake!

"Nah, I should be okay, but if it gets busy I'll give her a call. Everything okay?"

"Yep, everything's fine." It wasn't a total lie, but I didn't want to panic her. I had this heavy feeling in my chest, a sense of foreboding—I couldn't sit back and wait for Finn and Morgan to do whatever it was they were meant to be doing, I needed to take action. And I needed to find Jackson...where was he? Why wasn't he calling me back?

I drove by his house, but his car wasn't in the drive, so I continued to the police station. The frosty reception from Police Officer Liliana Miles wasn't unusual or unexpected. She'd never liked me and liked me even less now that I was going out with Jackson...her ex-boyfriend.

"He's not here," she snapped. As soon as she'd seen me walk through the door she'd suddenly become immensely interested in a stack of paperwork on the counter, refusing to look at me.

"Do you know when he'll be back?" I pressed.

"Nope."

"Do you know where he is?"

"Sorry, can't divulge his location to a civilian." She was being deliberately difficult and it rankled.

I was leaning in, ready to give her a piece of my mind, when Officer Philips rounded the corner and spotted me. "Oh hi, Harper," His smile was warm and friendly, in stark contrast to Liliana. "Looking for Jackson? He's not here. Got called to East Dondure on a case."

I blinked in surprise. "He did?"

"Yeah, last night. Something about an old case he and his partner had been working on."

"The one who got shot? Bryan?" Bryan had been the name Jackson had said last night.

"Yeah, I think that's him. Surprised Jackson didn't tell you."

"My phone died." I explained. "Well, I've left him a couple of voice mails but he's obviously busy." I didn't look at Liliana but knew she was listening to our conversation unabashedly. I'm sure she was delighted that Jackson had left town without telling me. "Thanks, Officer Philips."

"Not a problem, Harper, anytime."

I left the station even more confused—and hurt—than before. Not only did Jackson run out on me at dinner but now he'd left town altogether? Without a word.

"That's not like him," Jenna said when I called her from the car on my way to Drixworths.

"I know," I agreed. "But it still stings."

"Of course it does. Especially after what happened with Simon. But Jackson would never cheat on you."

I sighed, slowing to a stop at the junction of White and Penang. "I know that too. But I'm worried. Something seriously freaked him out last night. He saw something, something I couldn't see, and now he's gone to East Dondure?"

"You said he mentioned his dead partner's name last night? And Officer Philips just told you he's gone to East Dondure about a case he'd been working on with him. Correct?"

"That's right."

"So it's clearly work-related. And with the rift in the wards, maybe Jackson is seeing ghosts who have already passed. Maybe ghosts of murder victims? Or murderers!"

Looking left, then right, I pulled out. "You're probably right."

"You know it." I could hear the grin in her voice. Of course, she was right. It all made logical, perfect, sense. In which case, a thirty-second phone call telling me what was happening wasn't too much to ask, was it? Deciding I'd had enough of worrying about Jackson and why he hadn't called, I focused on our immediate problem. The broken ward that was letting demons into Whitefall Cove. That was at the crux of everything.

"Could you do me a favor?" I asked Jenna.

"On it." The sound of her fingers hitting the keyboard came down the line.

"I want to know more about Finn Hurley and Morgan Healy. Are they who they say they are? The wards should have been easy enough for them to repair, yet here we are, twenty-four hours later and supernatural entities are still crossing over."

"Way ahead of you, babe." Of course, she was. Jenna was a reporter; her mind was even more inquisitive than mine. "I'm writing up an expose on the whole thing."

"Of course you are." I smiled. "Did you know that Morgan is a descendant of the Queen of Avalon?"

"I do now. Can I quote you as a source?"

I chuckled. "No. I'm not the source. Llewellyn Cox the demon hunter told me. I want to know if it's true. He said she uses her supernatural gifts to manipulate people."

"The plot thickens," she murmured, fingers clicking on the keyboard. "I love my job." I could tell by her distracted tone that she was already busy following that particular lead. Time for me to follow up with Izzy. She knew more than she was letting on and I was determined to find out what.

CHAPTER
EIGHT

rixworths had always struck me as a place of calm—busy, but calm. Not today. Frantic activity abounded, with witches hurrying to and fro, wands aloft. Closing the large front door behind me, I glanced around, brows raised. The walls were covered with green goo. The substance slowly oozed down the wooden panels to pool in ever-growing puddles on the floor. To add to the chaos, a goblin-like creature was swinging from the chandelier, spitting out balls of slime. Each time a witch took aim with her wand he'd land a perfect shot, covering her in goop.

"Head down!" someone shouted, and I automatically ducked just in time to avoid one of the massive spitballs from landing on me. Reacting instinctively, I raised my hand and a pulse of magic shot through the air, freezing the goblin mid spit.

"You got him!" A short round witch with bright purple hair clapped in glee by my side. Keeping my eye on the goblin, I muttered out of the corner of my mouth, "Yeah well, now I don't know what to do with him—or how long my magic will hold."

"Not to worry. I've got this." And with a wave of her wand, the goblin creature disappeared.

"Was that a goblin?" I asked, dropping my hand and rolling my shoulders, a surge of adrenaline surging through me, making my body vibrate.

"Close." She began pointing her wand at the walls and zapping at the green slime, but just as quickly as she removed it from one spot, it came back somewhere else. "That was a gremlin."

I joined her in cleaning up the mess, but even with two of us at it, the green slime would not be stopped. "We need to find the source," I said. "This is getting us nowhere."

She nodded. "You're right. I'll go check upstairs." And off she went before I could stop her. With no immediate threat other than the slime, I decided my time was better spent searching for Izzy, finally finding her in a classroom at the rear of the building.

"Oh hey," she grunted, wand in one hand, a rope in the other. On the other end of the rope was a troll and they looked like they were playing a game of tug rope.

She'd heave it toward herself and the troll would dig in his heels before giving the rope a sudden jerk and almost pulling Izzy off her feet. For a troll, he was smart. He timed the sudden pulls on the rope for whenever she managed to lock him in the crosshairs of her wand. "Give me a hand, will ya?"

I repeated the same move I'd made on the gremlin, felt my magic shoot out of my fingertips and freeze the troll in place. "That's all I can do." I said, hand outstretched as I held him frozen.

"It's all I need," she assured me. With a wave of her wand, the troll disappeared, off to join the gremlin on the other side of the rift, I assumed.

Sliding her wand into her belt, Izzy dusted her hands and turned to me. "Thanks for your help."

"What on earth is going on?"

"The wards—" she began, but I cut her off.

"I know about the wards. It's why Finn and Morgan are here. And out of interest, where are they now? Why aren't they dealing with this?" I waved my arm around, indicating the chaos that had befallen Drixworths.

Izzy stiffened, eyes narrowing. "They are repairing the wards." I felt it, like nails on a blackboard, the jarring screech of a lie.

"Why is it taking so long?" I demanded, hurt at being lied to by someone I liked and trusted, but also frustrated at being stonewalled. "And why are all these creatures descending on Whitefall Cove? What's the attraction? Why do gremlins and goblins and trolls want to be here?"

"It's complicated." Crossing her arms, she turned, heading to the high arched windows, her back ramrod straight.

"I can do complicated," I said. "Try me." She remained silent while my mind chewed over what she'd said. "It's not the wards, is it?" It was a guess. A long shot. Repairing wards was a quick fix. Simple. It might need power that our citizens didn't have, but it wasn't difficult per se. It didn't make sense that our town was still besieged by demons and otherworldly creatures.

Throwing her hands up in the air, she spun. "Okay fine!" I didn't miss the slightly hysterical note in her voice. "It's not the wards. The township isn't even warded. It's a rift. There's a tear between dimensions and that tear is right in the middle of Whitefall Cove."

I knew my eyebrows had shot into my hairline, I could feel them, pulling my skin taut. I made a conscious effort to relax as I absorbed what she'd said. It made much more sense. And then I thought of something else.

"Did you spell us? At the town meeting? Did you spell us to believe your story about the wards?"

She had the grace to look ashamed.

"That's against the witches' law." I shook my head.

I'd run afoul of the rules myself in the past, had my witches license revoked because of it. I just couldn't believe Izzy would do such a thing.

"It was for everyone's protection. They needed to be aware that there was danger but not panic."

"Tell me about this rift." I knew nothing about multi-dimension activity, rifts, or tears. But clearly there were other worlds besides ours, and with some sort of opening between the two, our little town was being inundated by an unwanted population. Crazy thoughts ricocheted around in my brain like a pinball. I just needed a moment's peace to process it.

"Come into my office," Izzy said, and I followed her out of the classroom and into the familiar haven of her office. She took her seat behind her desk and things felt blissfully normal for one nanosecond.

"I assume Finn and Morgan are here to attempt to repair the tear in the dimensions?" I asked.

She nodded. "They are."

"And do we know how this happened?"

She shook her head. "We don't."

Right. So we had a hole between dimensions that was effectively allowing supernatural monsters into our world and we didn't know how to close it. "This rift...is it a one-way thing?"

"What do you mean?"

"I mean, these creatures are crossing over into our world, into Whitefall Cove. Has anyone traveled into their dimension? Is it even possible? Maybe the tear originated there."

Her face registered a combination of surprise and shock. "I hadn't thought of that," she admitted. "We can send them back through the rift, that much we know, but so far we've been unable to stop them from coming through in the first place."

"Finn is from another dimension. The Otherworld. Surely he knows more about this type of thing than any of us."

"That's why I requested his help." Izzy nodded. Her usually immaculate hair was showing signs of the day she'd had, strands sticking out from the blonde braid she wore, tendrils curling around her face. Flattering but far removed from the impeccably groomed witch I was used to seeing.

"And where are Finn and Morgan now?"

"They're in the basement."

"So they are here."

"Technically."

"But they don't know how to fix this, do they?" That was what was taking so long. The experts Izzy had brought in to help us had no clue. But I knew one person who might just be able to shed some light on the whole situation. Llewellyn Cox.

"Oh my Lord." I clapped my hand over my eyes and quickly turned my back. The demon hunter was as naked as a jaybird.

"Oh hey, Harper," he said, greeting me, not concerned in the least that I'd just caught him sans clothes. "What can I do for you?"

Flustered, I floundered, lost for words. He was spread out on a blanket laid in the grass behind his camp, head propped up on one elbow. As my eyes darted away I'd caught sight of an easel a few feet away, and a female figure behind it. Lord, I hoped it wasn't Gran.

He chuckled, then said, "Do you mind if we take a break, Vanessa?"

A sultry voice purred, "Sure, take five." I sagged in relief. Not Gran.

I longed to turn around and see who the woman was, but I didn't need another eyeful of Llewellyn in the buff, so I kept my back turned. I could hear movement, then Llewellyn drawled, "You can turn around. I'm decent."

I slowly swiveled my head to peek over my shoulder. Sure enough, he'd pulled on a pair of jeans. I conceded now was not the time to be prudish. I could ignore the fact that he had no shirt on. The woman named Vanessa was dressed in a white button-down shirt that was covered in paint stains, held closed by one button at her navel, revealing tantalizing glimpses of her flesh. Not to mention she wasn't wearing pants, just a long expanse of bare legs. She dropped the paintbrush she was holding into a jar of water and winked at me.

"Vanessa, this is Harper Jones, a local witch. Harper, this is Vanessa Howe, vampire." He introduced us while he dug around in a cooler, pulling out two cans of soda and tossing one at me. I was too busy staring at Vanessa to catch it and it hit me in the chest before bouncing to the ground.

"You're a vampire?" I stared at her incredulously. "How are you out in the sun?"

She smiled and I caught the unmistakable glint of fangs. "I'm also a sorceress. Cross heritage. Comes in handy."

"Need a drink, babe?" Llewellyn asked her. She crossed to him, ran a hand across his chest, leaned in close and licked his neck.

"You offering?" she purred, her nail caressing his carotid artery. I gulped.

Llewellyn laughed and swatted her on her behind. "Nope. I was thinking more along the lines of tea. I've got that herbal blend you like."

"Sure." She chuckled, turning her attention to me. "Nice to meet you, Harper."

"You too." I shook her proffered hand, surprised at how warm her flesh was. Vampires didn't freak me out, my best friend was one, but I was so used to

Monica being cold—and only coming out at night—that I was totally thrown for a loop.

"Dad was a vampire, Mom was a sorceress," Vanessa explained, "and I'm the result—a hybrid if you like."

Llewellyn held out a glass of iced tea to Vanessa. "She's a fab artist." He said, "Have you seen her work?"

I shook my head, couldn't say I had, but I had heard of her. Well, the name Howe that is. She had some paintings hanging in the Council offices.

"She paints in blood," Llewellyn continued, popping the top of his soda and taking a long swig.

"You do?"

"Among other mediums." She smiled, a warm, friendly smile. "Blood is my muse. I guess that's my vampiric heritage. I only use models who are okay with making a small donation."

"She mixes it with paint," Llewellyn added.

Vanessa chuckled. "Look at her face. She's appalled but curious."

I could feel the blood surge to my face, knew my cheeks must be red, but she wasn't wrong. I was curious and repulsed at the same time.

Llewellyn took pity on me. "Enough teasing. She's obviously here for a reason. How can I help?" Crossing to my side, he settled a hand on the small of my back and guided me a few steps away so Vanessa wouldn't overhear us.

"Shouldn't you be out, you know, demon-hunting?" The words blurted out with no filter, I was that rattled.

Seemed Llewellyn Cox wasn't a man easily offended. "Instead of lounging around in the nude having my portrait painted, you mean?" My cheeks were on fire with embarrassment. He barked out a laugh at my discomfort. "You are such a little prude. Which surprises me, given your relationship to Alice."

"Leave my Gran out of this," I grumbled.

"Fair enough. And to answer your question, I have been. Dealt with a demon at Vanessa's house an hour ago. This is her payment."

"Her painting a nude portrait is payment?"

"Sure! I accept any form of payment for services rendered. Vanessa asked if I'd like a portrait, I accepted."

"And whose idea was it for it to be a nude portrait?"

"Does it matter?"

He was right. It didn't. And it made no difference to me other than the fact that he was spot on with his assessment—I'm a prude and I was highly uncomfortable with the entire situation.

"Not in the least," I lied.

"So why are you here, Harper?"

"A couple of reasons. I want to ask about talismans —to protect us from demon possession."

"Not a foolproof method of protection, but certainly they can act as a deterrent to some degree." He nodded.

"I was wondering why, at the town meeting, it wasn't suggested to us that we use talismans."

He rubbed his chin. "I can't answer to that, but my guess is Tweedledum and Tweedledee didn't think it necessary."

I smirked at his reference to Finn and Morgan. "You had another reason for this visit?" he prodded.

"Yes. Last night, when you found me...was I possessed? Did you do an exorcism on me?"

His eyes widened in surprise. "What? No. Why? Is it the time thing? You were certainly confused and disoriented."

"Yeah...I just wondered if maybe that was why."

"Well, I can answer that one for you. No, you were not possessed." He paused, considering. "Maybe haunted?"

"Haunted?" I pounced on it, remembering the reflection I'd seen in the clothing store window. "That's a possibility? Ghosts can mess with time like that?"

"Not messing with time, messing with you. Who have you pissed off that they'd want to haunt you?"

The only ghost I knew was Whitney Sims and she haunted me in a friendly way. "I've no idea."

"I hear there's a necromancer in town. You should

look him up," Llewellyn suggested, taking another swig of his drink. I realized I'd left mine on the grass where it had fallen.

"He's out of town right now," I replied absently.

"Ahhh. But you know him?"

I nodded. "He's my boyfriend."

I could feel Llewellyn looking at me. "Is that right?" he murmured.

"What?"

"Nothing, nothing." He patted my shoulder. "How about I whip you up a talisman, hmmm?"

CHAPTER
NINE

Llewellyn led the way into his greenhouse. Now that he was set up at the park he'd propped open the sides of the trailer and the space was a lot bigger than I originally thought. I followed him inside, admiring the shelves upon shelves of pots all sporting plants of varying descriptions. I had my old research books back at the store and knew I could probably identify half a dozen of the herbs he had grown, although that wasn't necessary since he had little wooden stakes embedded in each pot with the name of the plant in neat handwriting.

"Mandrake, nightshade, hemlock..." I read out loud. "That's quite the collection."

"Trust you to go straight to the dangerous stuff." He smirked, picking up a pair of secateurs and snipping a small piece off a tall red plant, before moving to another.

Overhead, where the roof arched, pots hung by metal hooks, only at the very end, it wasn't a pot but a cauldron. Curious, I approached. "Why do you have a cauldron?" I asked. Llewellyn stopped what he was doing and looked at me.

"You can see that?"

I snorted. "Well yeah, it's right here." I reached up and knocked on the side of it with my knuckle. It was on the small side for a cauldron, but I knew one when I saw one, and this was most definitely a cauldron.

"Interesting." He continued with gathering a collection of herbs, then stepped down from the trailer. Outside he'd set up a workbench and through the open screen I watched him crush up the herbs he'd collected with a mortar and pestle, spread out a scrap of fabric and then wrap the crushed herbs in the fabric, securing it tightly with string. He held the little pouch up. "All set, come and get it."

The steps creaked as I joined him outside and accepted the talisman he'd made.

"It's not foolproof," he warned, dropping it into my palm, "but it should help keep the beasties away." The scent of the crushed herbs was sweet and filled the air around us. He was humoring me, and I wasn't sure if I should be annoyed or...I'm not sure what. Llewellyn was different from any man I'd met before. He reminded me of a female version of Gran and I wasn't sure if that was a good thing or bad. He dusted his hands on his jeans and cocked his head.

"Oh. Payment!" I began to rummage around in my bag, searching for my wallet.

He laughed. "Relax, Harper, it's not necessary."

"No, you said Gran's exorcism was a freebie."

"I did. But you don't need to pay me for the talisman. Forget it."

I paused. "This is no way to do business, Llewellyn," I told him. "How are you going to pay for the site hire? Keep the electricity on in your RV?"

"I manage just fine," he assured me, his lopsided grin quite disarming. "Was there anything else?" he prompted me when I stood there not saying anything.

"I was at Drixworths Academy this morning," I said, hand clutching the talisman in a death grip. "And Izzy tells me the town doesn't have a problem with—" I stopped, suddenly aware that we were out in the open, that anyone could potentially overhear what I was about to say.

Llewellyn dropped all pretense of charm and nodded once, curtly. "Come into the RV." Calling out to Vanessa, he yelled, "Vanessa, we're gonna have to take a rain check on the portrait, babe."

"I figured as much." Vanessa appeared in front of us, her vampiric speed startling me. She was still dressed in the paint-stained shirt and nothing else, but under her arm was the easel and in her other hand a battered case that I assumed she carried her art supplies in. "Call me when you want to pick this up again." With a wink, she was gone, a puff of air ruffling my hair.

The door to the RV was open and I climbed inside, automatically turned to the right, and settled myself into the seat I'd occupied yesterday. The RV rocked when Llewellyn climbed in. He turned left, towards the bed at the end, stopping to open his closet and pull a faded blue T-shirt over his head, before heading back to close the door.

"It's the rift," he said, taking a seat opposite me, leaning back with his ankle resting on the opposite knee, arm stretched over the back of the chair.

"You knew." I accused. He smirked. "I'm a hunter, a gypsy, and a mystic."

"Do you know how to fix it? Because I'm not convinced Finn and Morgan do."

His snort was derisive. "Those two are only here for their own gain."

"Which is?"

He lifted his shoulders. "No clue, but something self-serving I'm sure."

"So you're our only hope? Is that why Izzy contacted you?"

"She didn't."

"What?"

"Contact me."

"How are you here then?"

"Because I'm good at what I do." He uncrossed his legs and planted his feet on the floor, leaned forward so his elbows were resting on his knees and stretched out his back. "I pinpointed the rift when I was scrying, knew there was trouble in Whitefall Cove, and here I am."

"Right. So you've done this before?"

He gave a curt nod. "Once. It wasn't easy."

"But you can help? You can fix it."

"It's not like waving a magic wand and casting a spell. It's not that easy."

"What then?"

"We not only need to find out who created the rift, but why. Otherwise, we're going to be swimming against the tide—we fix it, they break it, and the cycle goes on."

"That's possible?" Then I remembered what I'd told Izzy. "Could this be originating from the other side? The other dimension?"

"Doubtful. They have no reason to be here. There's nothing for them in this world."

"Why are they crossing into it then?"

"Just for the pure joy of it. There's an open door that never used to be there. Let's go through it and see what's on the other side." The way he explained it made sense and I could see why the creatures were crossing over into Whitefall Cove.

"So you're saying whoever did it is in Whitefall Cove?"

Another curt nod. "Correct."

"How do we find them?"

"That's the difficult part. I can't get a trace on them until they use their magic and they've been quiet since I've been here."

Thoughts bounced around in my head. "I wonder why someone would do something like this?" I wondered out loud.

He wrinkled his nose. "Hard to say. Sometimes this type of thing happens by accident. Someone is trying to do something new, cast a spell they've never done before, and things go wrong. Other times it is intentionally dark and nefarious."

"But to open a door to another dimension...by accident...you'd have to be dabbling in black magic for that to happen? Right?"

"Yup." It wasn't the answer I wanted to hear. To think someone was practicing dark magic in Whitefall Cove sent a shudder down my spine.

I held up the talisman still clutched in my hand. "Is this a placebo?" What I really wanted to know was, was it going to protect me from the dark magic.

"Not at all. It will ward off dark and evil..."

"To a certain degree," I filled in for him.

"Agreed." He paused, then continued. "What we have here is a situation. The door to another world has been opened—and it remains open—which tells me that whoever is being summoned isn't here yet. All these other demons, the minors like the goblins, ghosts, and ghouls, are more a nuisance than anything else. But also a wonderful distraction for whoever is behind this, a very effective smokescreen. The energy in Whitefall Cove is off the charts, making it impossible for me to pinpoint the originating source. I'm not convinced that was intentional or a happy coincidence for whoever is behind this."

"But someone is behind it. And they're calling something...dark?" I shivered again. I'd been feeling it for the last two days. Something bad was coming. It was there, on the edge of my senses, niggling at me like a tiny splinter just under the skin.

"I'd say so."

"How do we close the rift then?" Because once we found who opened it, we had to close it.

"Let me worry about that."

I rolled my eyes. "Urgh. Don't fret. I'm not trying to steal your job! But wouldn't it make sense if I'm going to be helping you that I know what to do? What we'll need?"

"We?" His eyes widened in surprise.

"Well, yeah." Of course, I'd be helping him. We were in a bind—Izzy was busy with Finn and Morgan, who were appearing to be relatively useless in our precarious situation.

"I don't need help."

"Oh don't go all manly on me." I sighed. "Everyone needs help. This is my town. I have a coven of witches. Hell, we have two covens and for the sake of Whitefall Cove I'm sure we can work together for the greater good—just this once."

Llewellyn jumped to his feet, hands held out. "No! No covens. Heaven save me from a dozen witches!" His panic was exaggerated and for a second I thought he was serious. Then his lip twitched.

"Ha, ha," I grumbled, crossing my arms over my chest. "Very funny."

"Too easy." He sniggered, relaxing back in his seat. "No, but seriously, it's best I don't tell you too much."

"Why?"

"Because there is some very dark magic in play and if the person behind it suspects you're involved then they just might use it against you. And while you might be this powerful witch, you are pretty clueless and have no idea what you're doing with your powers."

My mouth fell open. "Oh." Yes, well, don't sugar coat it or anything. His reference to my lack of prowess in the magic department stung.

"How do you even know that if you're not a witch?" I grumbled.

He sighed, shaking his head. "Not everyone who uses magic is a witch. You have a very limited viewpoint."

"I only know what I know," I protested.

"It wasn't a criticism, just an observation. Calm down."

"So you think you can help?"

"With your magic? Absolutely. But we'd have to do it on the down-low."

"Why? Do you think Izzy would get upset?" Izzy had been meeting with me for months to help train me in the use of my magic, although to be honest, I had blown off our last three sessions.

"I don't care about Izzy's feelings," he assured me. "I care about keeping your ass alive."

I gasped, truly shocked at his words. "Alive? What, my magic can kill me now?"

"You truly are naive." He shook his head, the expression on his face was incredulous. "For an intelligent woman, you are not connecting the dots. There is someone in Whitefall Cove dabbling in dark magic. They are trying to either resurrect someone from the dead or pull through a demon or something equally disastrous—and they are darn close to succeeding. Then we have you. A failed witch with a lot of power at her disposal and limited knowledge on how to use it. So, we start training you. And you learn to use, harness, command the power that is yours. And now there is a great big target on your back because the type of power you have at your fingertips just might be what they need to complete the job."

The RV was eerily silent. I swallowed, a loud gulp. He was right and why hadn't I thought of that? Because I was a failed witch. He'd said it. Not to be mean, but a truth. A truth I needed to accept before I could move on.

"We train in secret?" I asked.

He nodded. "We train in secret."

"Can I tell Jackson?"

"The necromancing boyfriend who's mysteriously disappeared?" The way he said it sounded bad. But Jackson wasn't behind this, I was sure of it. He shook his head. "No."

"Gran?" I asked hopefully.

He shook his head again. "Nope. No one. It's not that I don't trust them, it's more that they might accidentally let something slip. This has to stay between us. If you can't manage that, then don't bother."

It was the first time anyone had truly left the decision to me. Ever since my return to Whitefall Cove I'd been told over and over what I had to do with my magic. I was a powerful witch, I had to do this, I had to do that, but Llewellyn was offering up a tantalizing alternative. Don't bother. Something shriveled within at the thought.

"I can't turn my back on my magic," I whispered.

He grinned. "I know." Before I could respond he held up a hand to shush me. "Hunter. Gypsy. Mystic." In other words, stop questioning everything and accept what I know to be true. Easier said than done.

CHAPTER

TEN

"Sorry. Am I keeping you awake?" Sarcasm rolled off my tongue as I eyeballed Llewellyn who was laid out on the bench behind the lighthouse, one arm slung over his eyes. We'd been meeting here daily, training in secret. I'd learned more from him in one day than what I had at Drixworths in a year! Why wasn't he teaching there? After all of this was over I'd ask Izzy. Although technically Llewellyn wasn't a witch, he brought so much more to the table surely they wouldn't refuse?

He'd been very interested when I'd told him I could astral walk. He'd agreed that could come in handy for what was ahead. But I also knew where all this training was ultimately leading. Levitation. He was convinced I was the Whitelight Witch and I was starting to think maybe he was right because last night when I was collapsed on the sofa from exhaustion, I'd been too tired to reach for the remote on the coffee table. The next thing I knew, it was in my hand. I'd been so surprised I'd dropped it, but when I tried again, it didn't work. I'd yet to tell him that, wanted to keep it as a surprise until I'd learned to control it. Okay, I admit it, I wanted to show off.

"In case you hadn't noticed, Ms. Jones," he drawled, "I'm a busy man, in-between working with you and rift patrol, I mean. That's a non-stop job."

I snorted. "Word around town is you've been indulging in some extracurricular activities." It was true though, Llewellyn had been busy. He'd set a series of traps around town, designed to send any supernatural creature that got caught in it, back through the rift. But they had to be re-set constantly, not to mention he was still trying to pinpoint who was behind the rift. Gran had told me that she'd dropped by to visit him late one night and his RV had been rocking in a way that screamed do not disturb. I was curious about who his romantic liaison was.

Lifting his arm a fraction he peered at me. "Is that right?"

I was practicing calling forth weather elements and held balanced between my hands a small rain cloud. It gave off a little rumble of thunder and I grinned. It was the cutest little thing and I eyed Llewellyn, considered dumping the load of rain the little cloud held over his head, but as soon as I'd thought of it, he'd raised a hand and flicked his own magic my way and now I stood dripping.

"Hey!" I protested, immediately drying myself. "What was that for?"

"Pft. You are as transparent as a pane of glass, Jones." He went back to relaxing on the bench. Archie, who was sprawled across his stomach, lifted his head to peer at us, uttered a sleepy meow as if asking us to keep the noise down, before dozing off again. "Sorry, buddy," Llewellyn apologized, patting him. The resulting purr rumbled loudly.

"Traitor," I teased.

"Try something bigger," Llewellyn mumbled, voice muffled.

"Bigger?"

"You're playing small. Try the ocean."

I turned, eyeballed the blue sea behind us. Could I manipulate the ocean? In the past, I would have been reluctant to try in case I failed, but one thing Llewellyn had taught me was that I was capable of pretty much anything I put my mind to. I just had to believe. Standing on the bluff, the wind blowing my hair back from my face, I held my arms outstretched, closed my eyes and concentrated. I pictured slowly swirling the sea into a whirlpool, then lifting it to dance in the sky. When I cracked open an eye I gasped in surprise.

"Easy," Llewellyn warned. "Don't lose focus or this

could end badly. You don't want to harm anyone—on land or in the water."

I immediately thought of all the fish I'd inadvertently scooped up into the waterspout that was now madly spinning around. Okay, I can do this. I slowed the spin and gently, slowly, lowered the waterspout back into the ocean, calmly, without triggering a tsunami.

"I did it!" I glanced over my shoulder at Llewellyn. He was sitting up now, Archie on his lap while he kept a close eye on me. I wanted to jump up and down with excitement, pleased with myself, but most of all? I wanted to tell Jackson. He'd be so proud. He'd insist we celebrate. Only there had been no word. Every day I called and it went straight to voice mail. I didn't know what to think. Was he ignoring me or was he that busy with his case that he couldn't take a few seconds to call, or at least text, to let me know he was okay?

"Whoa, what are you thinking about?"

"What?" I blinked, bringing my mind back to Llewellyn.

"Your face was like a thundercloud. What's on your mind?" Lifting Archie off his lap and onto the bench by his side, he crossed to my side, looking out over the bay of Whitefall Cove.

I sighed. Was it that obvious? "Nothing," I lied.

He rested a hand on my shoulder but remained silent. "I've got to go reset the traps. Wanna come?"

A distraction was exactly what I needed. I nodded.

Two hours later we were back at the trailer park, the traps had been reset. Llewellyn had been so pleased with my progress I was now solely in charge of three traps and I had to admit I liked the feeling of pride it gave me. But there was also a pang of guilt as I drove past the closed doors of The Dusty Attic that evening. I'd been so busy with training and demon hunting with Llewellyn that I'd had little time for anything else. Wendy had assured me she had the bookstore under control, but I was acutely aware that she had a baby at home to care for and our initial agreement was that she'd work for me on a part-time basis, yet she'd been at the store from nine to five for the last few days. I was pondering calling Gran and asking her to take a couple of shifts when I pulled into the car park and made my way to Llewellyn's RV. He was standing by the door waiting for me, a note clutched in one hand, a look of disbelief on his face.

"Did you complain about me?" he demanded.

I looked at him. "Are you for real? Why would I complain about you? And to whom? About what?" I protested. He thrust the note into my hand and stormed into the RV. I smoothed out the crumpled paper and read it. An eviction notice from the trailer park. Nudity complaints. He was to vacate by tomorrow.

"It wasn't me," I said, following him into the RV. "It was days ago when I stumbled across you posing for Vanessa," I pointed out. "Why would I complain now?"

Rubbing a hand around the back of his neck he nodded. "You're right. Sorry."

"Who else has seen you naked?" I chuckled, it was such an odd thing to say, but with Llewellyn, it was perfectly normal.

He smirked. "Could be anyone. I like to be nude." I rolled my eyes. So did my Gran. She'd had public indecency warnings before.

"Anyone today?"

"Actually..." He tapped his chin, deep in thought. "I was in the greenhouse this morning when those old biddies who own the tea shop dropped by."

"Poppy and Hetty?"

"That's them." He nodded. "Bought up big for their tea shop."

I remembered they said they were intending to buy some herbs from him for The Tea Leaf. "And were you wearing clothes?" I prompted.

He grinned, shaking his head. "I was not. But"—he held up a hand in protest—"I did grab an empty pot to cover myself with. To protect their modesty, not mine."

"It's likely it was them then." Although I doubted it was Hetty. She didn't seem as high strung as her sister. I could see Poppy complaining that Llewellyn was outside, naked, even though he was minding his own business and it was them who'd called in on him uninvited. It was hardly his fault, but I doubt Poppy saw it that way.

"They had an odd request," he told me now, putting the kettle on to make tea.

"Oh?"

"Yeah, they wanted to know if I could procure a magic cauldron for them."

I blinked. "A magic cauldron? Is there such a thing?"

He shook his head. "Not technically."

"You have a cauldron though, hanging in the greenhouse. Did they mean that?"

He glanced at me with narrowed eyes. "That is a magical cauldron, yes. And so far, aside from me, you are the only one who can see it."

"What? How?"

"Exactly." He sighed, busied himself with two mugs, creating yet another concoction for me to try. I'd never been a tea drinker, but Llewellyn was determined to convert me. Every day he'd come up with something different for me to try.

"Okay, let's break this down. First thing...you have

a magical cauldron. How is it magical and why do you have it?"

"It's been in my family for generations. A great-great-something or other was a witch and it belonged to her. She spelled it when the great witch hunt was on, to hide her secret. She died without lifting the spell, so now only members of my family can see it. And now you."

"But I'm not a member of your family." Oh my God, what if we were related?

"No, but you are the Whitelight Witch. I'm sure of it."

I chewed on my lip, debated telling him about my tiny display of telekinesis.

"Anyway, the cauldron has been hanging in my greenhouse for years. I haven't needed to use it, but it's safe enough there."

"So how would the Oliver sisters even know about it?"

"Good question." He turned, held out a steaming mug of tea to me, which I accepted, taking a deep sniff of the steam wafting up into my face. I cocked my brow. It smelled like marshmallows, yet looking down into the black brew, there wasn't a marshmallow in sight.

I took a tentative sip. Not bad. Not coffee, but not bad.

"You like?" he asked.

"It's okay."

He laughed. "I'm never going to win with you, Jones."

I smiled, taking another sip, while my mind mulled over the possibilities.

"I've got the solution to one of your problems," I said. "You can park your RV out at the cottage. There's plenty of space and you won't disturb anyone. Only one rule."

"Don't walk around naked?" he guessed, sounding dejected.

"How about, don't come into the cottage naked?"

"I can manage that." He smiled, white teeth flashing. I had a feeling Gran was suddenly going to be spending a lot of time at my house once she learned Llewellyn was living there too. Not to mention whoever he was hooking up with. And the various townsfolk who dropped by to buy his herbs and potions. Things were about to get busy at the lighthouse.

"Well. Welcome. Come on up in the morning. And I'm sorry the Oliver sisters got you evicted."

He tossed his hair. "Everything has a way of working out."

Finishing my drink, I set my cup on the sink. "See you in the morning."

"See you. And, Harper?"

I paused in opening the door, glancing back.

"Thank you. You didn't have to offer me a place to stay."

I smiled. "It's not a problem." I waved goodbye, my mind once again occupied by a million different thoughts. Yet again Jackson was front and center and I was seriously considering jumping in my car and driving to East Dondure to track him down. Only I couldn't do that while Whitefall Cove was in trouble. That led me to the Oliver sisters and their request for a magic cauldron. That was odd. Did they know Llewellyn had one? And if so, how? And what did they need it for? If they were behind this madness I couldn't let them know I was on to them by asking outright. I had to be sneaky about it, and if there was one thing I'd learned from Gran, it was how to be sneaky.

CHAPTER
ELEVEN

Llewellyn didn't turn up in the morning. Standing on my front porch, I sipped my coffee, kept half an eye on Archie, who was doing his usual hole digging routine, and half an eye on the private road leading to my cottage. Where was he? I'd promised Wendy the morning off, so it was my turn to open the store and after taking advantage of her for the last three days there was no way I could renege on that deal now. Not that I needed to be here, I sighed, it was just that Llewellyn would need access to the cottage, to use the bathroom, and I didn't want to leave the place unlocked. I pulled my phone from my back pocket and checked it for the millionth time. I'd already called him once and left a voice mail. He hadn't returned the call. Again it wasn't that odd. Llewellyn kept to his own routine of pretty much doing what he wanted when he wanted. He was probably still asleep.

Archie finished his business and joined me on the porch, rubbing around my ankles. Draining my coffee, I bent to scratch his ears. "Come on, boy, let's drop by and see what Llewellyn is up to and then go to the store. I can give him the spare key at least and you'll see him tonight when we get home."

Archie settled into his seat on the passenger side and within minutes I was pulling up at the trailer park. The RV sat in its usual spot, showing no signs that he intended to leave this morning. I frowned. Even the greenhouse trailer was wide open. I'd have thought he would have closed it all up ready to relocate. Archie, in great anticipation of seeing his new friend, trotted ahead of me. The side door to the RV was closed so Archie ducked under the vehicle and out the other side—the side where Llewellyn liked to lounge around naked. Archie's blood-curdling meow set the hairs on my arms on end.

"Archie?" I broke into a run, skidding around the front of the RV only to stumble to a halt at what I saw. Archie was meowing and making pitiful howling noises, pushing his nose into the crook of Llewellyn's neck and shoulder. Only Llewellyn didn't respond. Couldn't respond. I was pretty sure he was dead. Sucking in my breath, I tiptoed closer. He lay flat on his back in the grass, naked as a jaybird, his skin a pale shade of grey. His eyes, once a startling green, were now glazed and cloudy and staring sightlessly at the sky above.

"Llewellyn?" I croaked, crouching by his side. I pressed two fingers against his neck, searching for a pulse, knowing I wouldn't find one...his skin was cold to the touch.

"Mrooooooooow?" Archie cried mournfully. "Sorry, buddy," I whispered, my eyes filling with tears. "We've lost him." I swear to God Archie had tears in his eyes too. I scooped him up and hugged him tightly, needing a moment to gather myself. Llewellyn's wasn't the first dead body I'd found, but this was the first time someone I considered a friend had died. My eyes narrowed as I stood holding Archie and looking at Llewellyn's body. There, on his wrist...two puncture marks and a cut.

"What's this?" I muttered, lowering Archie to the ground. I crouched over the body for a closer look. The puncture wounds were small, round, with clean edges, yet the cut that ran through them made no sense. That too was clean, surgical precision clean. Not big, just a small slice, yet there was no blood. My eyes traveled from his face to his wrist, and back again.

Llewellyn had been drained of blood. It would explain the color of his skin. Grey. Bloodless. Was this a vampire attack? If it was, it was pretty neat. One small bite to the wrist. No tearing. If he'd been bitten against his will, there would have been damage, torn skin, and bruising. Unless he'd been rendered unconscious first. But the cut? A vampire wouldn't need to slice his wrist open to drink. And it wasn't self-harm or a suicide attempt, as the cut ran the wrong way.

"Doubtful," I said to Archie, who was watching with interest. "He's a demon hunter. Wouldn't be easy to subdue him." Crouching low, I studied the grass around him. Trampled on and flattened. Could have been one person or multiple; it was impossible to say, and since Llewellyn had used this area as his outdoor living room I doubted I'd find anything useful. Straightening, I headed to the greenhouse and stuck my head inside. Nothing appeared out of place. My eyes alighted on the cauldron. Still there, invisible to everyone except me. On the floor of the greenhouse was a sprinkling of herbs, but they could have been dropped by Llewellyn himself. He was in and out of the greenhouse constantly.

That left the RV. I knew I had to call the police before anyone else turned up and saw Llewellyn's body. But first I needed to check for clues. Llewellyn was murdered, and if there was one thing I knew how to do, that was how to catch a killer.

Stepping inside the RV, it hit me immediately, the faint smell of perfume in the air. I lifted my nose, closed my eyes, and dragged in a deep breath. It was oh, so familiar. Opening my eyes, I glanced at his rumpled bed, indentations in both pillows. His lady friend had been here last night. Two wine glasses sat in the sink, a deep red lipstick mark on one of them. My eyes zeroed in on the lipstick. The perfume? It smelled like the sultry musk that Monica wore. And that lipstick? The dark red that she favored.

"Oh, Monica...what have you done?" I whispered, worried for my vampire friend.

Something else was wrong though. His stuff was moved about. I'd been in here enough to know the order of the jars of herbs he kept on the counter...were out of order. The closet door stood ajar and I opened it further with my boot, careful not to leave fingerprints. I couldn't say for certain, but it looked like someone had rifled through Llewellyn's clothes. Or maybe he was just messy, but I doubted it. Considering the way he kept the rest of his RV, he didn't strike me as the type to stuff his clothes willy nilly into the closet.

The sound of my phone ringing was loud in the silence and I jumped, fumbled to pull it out of my back pocket. A glance at the screen had my eyebrows rising.

"Jackson?" I hadn't heard from him in days, yet the moment I find a dead body, he calls? One last glance around the RV and I made my way back outside, standing by Llewellyn's body. Archie had remained with him and my heart hurt for my poor cat who was going to miss his new friend.

"Harper. I'm so sorry. I just got caught up—"

"It doesn't matter." I cut him off. Yes, I wanted to hear him explain why he'd cut off all contact with me —and it had better be good—but right now I had more important things to worry about. "I need you."

He sighed. "I need you too, babe," he breathed into the phone.

"No," I snapped, "not in that way." Okay, yes, in that way, but now was not the time. And I was mad at him. He wasn't going to get off that easy.

"What's wrong?"

"Besides you disappearing for days on end without a word?" The words tumbled out before I could stop them. "I'm here at Llewellyn Cox's RV. He's been murdered."

You could have heard a pin drop. Seconds ticked by. I was digesting the fact that Jackson was back and he was digesting the fact that I was involved in another crime. Perfect.

"You're at the trailer park?" He was back, full cop mode.

"I am."

"On my way."

I didn't get a chance to answer; I was listening to the dial tone. I glanced down at Archie. "Here we go again, boy." I sighed, crossing my arms over my chest, and settled in to wait.

It didn't take long. Jackson appeared, a patrol car

following behind. I squinted into the morning light, watching as they crossed the park to where I waited, breathing a sigh of relief that it wasn't Officer Miles who accompanied Jackson, but Officer Philips.

"This way." I pointed to behind the RV. Jackson drew level with me, paused, his eyes running over me from top to toe, sending a tingle down my spine. I wanted nothing more than to launch myself into his arms and let him hold me. But this was neither the time nor the place, and before we got to any of that mushy cuddly stuff, he had some explaining to do.

He knew it, could read me like a book. His grin, accompanied by the adorable dimple I loved, made my heart melt. Damn it, he was pulling out all the stops and all he'd done was smile at me.

"Up to your neck in it again, Jones?" he drawled.

"Apparently."

He matched his stride to mine as we rounded the RV. Llewellyn was exactly where I'd left him, which was no surprise considering he was dead. Officer Philips was talking into the radio clipped to his shoulder.

"Tell me what happened," Jackson said, eyes sweeping the area, missing nothing.

I filled him in, leaving nothing out. Nothing except I had a sinking suspicion the woman Llewellyn had been seeing was Monica. A vampire. And coincidentally Llewellyn had been drained of blood. At least I was pretty sure he had. A wave of nausea rolled through me at the thought.

"He was moving into your place?" Jackson's tone told me he was taken aback with that piece of news.

I folded my arms across my chest. "He was moving his RV to my place," I corrected.

"Why?"

"Because he'd been asked to leave the trailer park," I said.

"Why?"

I blew out a breath. "Someone made a complaint—I suspect it was one of the Oliver sisters—about his public nudity."

Jackson's eyebrows shot up. "His what?" The eyebrows lowered into a frown. I could see him connecting the dots.

"It's nothing like that," I grumbled. "Llewellyn was a bit of a free spirit, liked to be at one with nature and all of that stuff. He actually reminded me of a male version of Gran. Too bad you weren't around to get to know him yourself." The last part slipped out with a high degree of snark. Yep. Still annoyed with him.

"Explain to me the naked part again."

"Why? Too late to charge him with public indecency. Despite the fact that he was in his own home, minding his own business."

"This is a public place—I take it he was parading

around out here? In the nude." He waved a hand at the naked body behind us.

"He wasn't parading around. The first time he was posing for a nude portrait. Vanessa Howe was painting him."

He skipped over that and zeroed in on what snagged his attention the most. "The first time?"

Exasperated, I planted my fists on my hips and glared at him. "Will you stop fixating on the fact that he liked to get around without any clothes on? Someone killed him, Jackson. As in dead. And like it or not, he was helping me." I lowered my voice. "With my magic. I learned more from him in the last couple of days than I did with weeks of lessons at Drixworths."

Jackson studied me for a moment, then rested a hand on my shoulder. "He was your friend." It wasn't a question.

"He was." I sniffed. I remembered the first time I'd met Llewellyn and Gran's subsequent exorcism and not knowing what to think of the gypsy demon hunter who'd rolled into town. I'd thought him to be a womanizer and possibly a fraud, but he'd proved me wrong. I cleared my throat and squared my shoulders. "I was helping him with the traps."

"Traps?"

"You really need to get up to speed on what's been happening here since you've been gone." My snark was back. With exaggerated patience, I filled him in.

"Whitefall Cove does not have a ward problem, it has a rift problem, and until the rift is closed, beasties from another dimension are going to keep crossing over. Llewellyn set up a series of traps around town to catch and dispatch them back to where they came from. He taught me how to reset the traps. Which"—I glanced up at the sky—"I'm guessing haven't been done this morning."

"He's been dead for hours, I'd say." Officer Philips approached. I'd seen him out of the corner of my eye, taking photos of the scene.

"Thanks, Philips," Jackson said. "Grab your gear and begin processing the scene. I want a bag over both of those hands too, preserve any evidence."

"The wound is an interesting one." Officer Philips told him. "Haven't seen anything like it before."

Jackson crossed to the body and crouched, examining the injury to Llewellyn's wrist. He glanced up at me. "What do you make of this?"

I frowned and chewed my lip. "It's like two separate wounds. Two round punctures, but then a straight cut as well. I don't know what could have done that."

"Hmmm." For someone so concerned about Llewellyn's naked status, he certainly wasn't in any hurry to cover the poor man's body. I turned my back, pondering how someone could have gotten the jump on him, half-listening to the movements behind me as the two men worked the scene. I moved out of the way when the coroner's van turned up, then suddenly remembered I was meant to open the store this morning.

"Shit," I muttered. Pulling out my phone, I glanced at the time. Nine thirty. Not that it mattered, I supposed, people were never lined up outside waiting to get in. I called Jackson over. "Can I go? I've got to open the store. I can come to the station later to give a statement."

His eyes held mine for an endless moment before he nodded. "Sure. I assume you've been in the RV?"

I nodded. "Yes."

His lips flattened into a straight line. "Great."

"And by that you mean I'm a suspect. Again." I glanced around, searching for Archie, found him lying in the sun at the front of the RV, watching the proceedings with interest. "You have my prints on file. You will find them inside. Probably my DNA too, I'm sure I've shed a strand of hair or two."

"Just how often have you been inside?" he asked.

"Daily. Pretty much. He was trying to find a blend of tea that I'd actually like. So far he'd been unsuccessful and now I guess we'll never know."

I walked away, calling Archie who jumped up and followed. "Time to call the murder club to order," I told him as we drove away.

CHAPTER
TWELVE

News about Llewellyn's death spread quickly, and panic ensued. Everyone assumed a demon had taken his life, but I suspected it was nothing of the sort. A demon didn't cut your wrist and drain you of blood. His blood was key...why would someone want it? The logical explanation was a vampire. Did Vanessa Howe need more to finish the portrait? But she'd said she only took a drop and mixed it with her paints. And when I'd seen them together, when she was painting his portrait, he'd shown no signs of injury. The blood she'd used had to have been from a pinprick. The other alternative was she'd needed his blood for sustenance. Did she even drink blood? She was a hybrid, she'd dodged the vampire curse of being allergic to the sun, but what about the blood for food thing?

I was avoiding thinking about the other, obvious, vampire in this equation. Monica. I chewed my lip as I reluctantly faced the truth. I was reasonably sure it was Monica's perfume I'd smelled, and her lipstick on the glass. Would the police be able to put that together? I didn't know. But if they were looking for a vampire to pin the murder on, she'd be one.

"Gadzooks, the world has gone crazy!" Gran burst through the door, slamming it shut behind her. Today's outfit consisted of daisy duke shorts over fishnet stockings, and a plaid pink and white shirt tied at her waist. A neon pink cowboy hat sat upon her head, the requisite Ugg boots on her feet. I wondered if her feet ever got hot in those, considering she practically wore them all year long.

"Yeeha!" I greeted. It had been slow in the bookstore today and I was sitting behind the desk we used as a counter, not doing much of anything other than pondering Llewellyn's murder. It was so quiet even Whitney hadn't put in an appearance, which was odd because she always seemed to turn up whenever I was in the store, keen to gossip.

"I hear that sexy demon hunter had his guts sucked out!" Gran declared, crossing to the coffee pot, pouring herself a cup and then promptly spitting it back out. "Gross," she grumbled.

I shook my head. "You heard wrong." Gran hopped up onto the side of the desk, legs swinging. "You found him, didn't you? Folks have been making a bit of noise about that."

"I don't care what people say," I lied. I totally cared what people said or thought about me. Even I was becoming a little suspicious over my propensity to find dead bodies. Was I a dead body magnet?

"Bull hockey." Gran slapped my wrist, hard. I flinched, moving out of her reach. "I know you care, child, don't be lying to me."

"Sorry."

"I should think so. Now. Tell me everything."

I filled her in, leaving out the part about Monica. I needed to talk to my friend alone first. I didn't think she'd done this, but she was involved. Gran listened intently, for once in her life not interrupting every few seconds. After I'd finished speaking a slow grin spread across her weathered face.

I didn't trust that smile. "What?"

"You know what this means, don't you?" The grin widened, showing her teeth.

"What?"

"The Murder Club is back in business!" She clapped her hands and bounced off the desk in excitement. I rolled my eyes. Trust Gran to be excited about a murder. But she was right. I was dying to close the store and reveal the clue board that was magically hidden behind a bookcase. Only a couple more hours until closing time and then I could. I worked better when I got all of my jumbled thoughts out of my head and onto the board.

"Sure." I indulged her, hoping I wouldn't regret it. "But not until after work."

"Yeah, yeah, yeah." She waved a hand as if my livelihood was of no consequence. "I'm going across to Bean Me Up for a decent coffee." She threw a withering glance at the coffee pot on the dresser in the middle of the store. "I'll be back at closing time." She punctuated with a fart and I waved her away, fanning the door to try and clear the air. What is it with old ladies farts? They could strip the paint off the walls. Even Archie, who was sleeping in an armchair in the corner, rolled over and tucked his head under his paw.

"Almost as bad as the goblins," I muttered, easing back into my chair. I picked up my phone, pulled up Monica's number, and dialed. She answered just before it rang out.

"'Ello?"

"I woke you. Sorry."

"'S'kay," she mumbled. "Gimme a sec."

I heard her put the phone down, background noise, then she was back. "Okay. I'm awake. What's up?" she asked, sounding wide awake and alert as if I hadn't just woken her from sleep mere seconds ago.

"I need to talk to you." I bit my lip, not knowing how to broach this.

"Now's your chance, we're talking now?" I could hear the smile in her voice.

"You may not have heard yet, but...Llewellyn Cox is dead." Way to sugar coat it, Harper. Silence on the other end of the line. I waited, knew she was processing. I listened to the ticking of the clock on the back wall of the store. *Tick, tick, tick.*

"How?"

"This isn't official, but from what I saw, it looked like he'd been drained of blood," I told her.

"You found him?"

I nodded, then remembered she couldn't see me. "I did. He was meant to move his RV out to my place this morning, but when he didn't turn up I figured I'd drop by and give him my spare key."

"He mentioned he was moving," she said absently.

I pounced. "Monica? Were you and Llewellyn seeing each other?"

She snorted. "What makes you ask that?" But I could hear the hint of defensiveness in her voice.

"Because I could smell your perfume in his RV this morning, and I saw your lipstick on a wine glass in his sink."

"Shit," she muttered.

"So you were?" I pushed.

She sighed. "Yes, okay, we were."

"Monica...were you drinking his blood?" I cringed at having to ask.

"What? No." She sounded affronted that I'd suggest such a thing. "I don't drink human blood, you know that. I only drink synthetic."

"Yes, I know," I told her. "I just wondered, you know, in the heat of the moment..." I trailed off.

"That I bit him?" she asked incredulously. "No. I did not. Ever." Then she came back with, "Is that how he died? Was he bitten?"

I shook my head. "Not bitten," I assured her. "But drained of blood."

"Oh, so you thought because he'd been drained of blood it must have been me," she snapped, her hurt clear.

"No, I didn't think that at all," I protested. "But the police are going to figure out you've been in his RV, that you were sleeping with him and they're going to ask the same questions." Then I added, "If it helps any, I'm a suspect too."

"You are?"

"Mmmhmm. I found the body. I've been in his RV multiple times. Fingerprints and DNA are going to show up."

It was her turn to pounce. "DNA? Were you shagging him too?" Her tone told me she wasn't happy about that prospect.

"No!" Our roles were reversed and it was my turn to protest. "For one, I'm with Jackson and I would never cheat on him! And two, Llewellyn and I were working together—surely he told you about it? I've been in his RV but not in his bed. Just to be clear."

"Funny enough we didn't talk about you when we were together," Monica said. "We had other...things...on our minds." Right. Like sex.

"Was it serious?" I asked, feeling bad for my friend.

"No. But it was fun. Llewellyn was never going to stick around so there were no expectations." She had a point. He was here to hunt demons, help fix the rift, and then he'd be moving on. Any dalliances he indulged in would not be lasting.

"Well, once I've closed up shop the Murder Club will be in session," I told her.

"I'll be there." There was none of Gran's delight in her tone, but then this was Monica's first time being on the suspect board.

Thunder rumbled and a bolt of lightning forked down from the sky with a crack. Standing at the window, I watched the storm roll in, the light fading as giant black clouds loomed overhead.

"Wraow, mrur," Archie complained in his sleep, tucking himself into a tighter ball on the chair, his head barely visible.

A big fat raindrop hit the footpath outside, a second later another, then another. I squinted through the window to Bean Me Up directly opposite, hoping to see Gran. She'd better get her butt here soon or she'd be caught in the deluge that was about to be unleashed. Too late. No sooner had I thought it than the heavens opened and the rain fell in a heavy sheet.

"May as well close up," I said to Archie. "No one is coming out in this." No one was coming in any way...I hadn't had a single customer all afternoon. Flipping the sign to closed, I caught sight of movement outside, a shadowy figure darting across the street. I held open the door and stood back as Gran torpedoed inside, soaked to the bone.

"Dad-sizzle, but it's raining cats and dogs out there!" She gasped, shaking herself, flinging drops of water everywhere. Absently I waved my hand at her, drying her off. I closed the door and flicked the lock, turned to find her looking at me with her mouth hanging open. "What?" I frowned.

"You did...that"—she waved her hand around in the air—"without even looking at me. And without that look of concentration on your face like you're about to take a poop."

I snorted. "Thanks. I think."

Her eyes narrowed. "You've been practicing."

"I already told you, I've been working with Llewellyn."

She nodded, a vigorous up and down motion. "You did, you did. I just didn't think you were..."

It was my turn to narrow my eyes. "You didn't think I was...what?"

She had the grace to look just a smidge ashamed.

"I thought practicing magic was a euphemism," she admitted.

"Gran! I wasn't sleeping with Llewellyn if that's what you were thinking. Geez. What is it with people in this town?" I grumbled, storming over to the coffee pot and pouring the last of the dregs into a cup. I bolted it down in one gulp and was just setting the cup down when a loud banging came from the front door. Whoever it was had a raincoat pulled over their head to protect them from the rain. Hurrying across, I flicked the lock and held the door open.

"Phew." Monica shot past me, shrugging out of her coat and hanging it on the coat hook to dry. "This storm is something else."

"Hey." I greeted her, closing the door again only to have a foot shoved into the gap between the door and frame to stop it from closing. I looked up to see Jenna pushing her way inside.

"Figured you'd be meeting." She shook off her umbrella. "And the storm would give Monica good coverage."

"Sharp as ever." I grinned.

"The gang's all here." Gran clapped her hands. "Let's get this show on the road."

"Is Jackson coming?" Jenna asked.

I shook my head. "I haven't told him we're meeting. There's some stuff we should talk about first."

"Ooooh, juicy." Gran rubbed her hands together in anticipation.

"Gran. This is serious."

"Yes, yes, I know. Continue." She waved her hand impatiently and I sighed in resignation. With a snap of my fingers, the blinds lowered, keeping prying eyes out, and the bookcase silently slid to one side, revealing the empty clue board behind it.

I crossed to the board, caught the pack of Post-it notes Monica tossed me, and picked up the marker left on the shelf at the bottom of the board from the last time we'd used it. Seemed to me we were using it a lot these days. I wrote Llewellyn's name on a Post-it and pinned it to the top of the board.

"Llewellyn Cox," I said, "was drained of his blood."

CHAPTER
THIRTEEN

Jenna's and Gran's heads swiveled to Monica, who frowned, then said to me, "See? As soon as you mention blood everyone thinks the vampire did it."

"Did the vampire do it?" Gran asked, crossing her arms and pinning Monica with what I called her interrogating stare. I bit my lip, fully expecting Monica to lose her cool, but she surprised me by chuckling and shaking her head.

"I did not."

Gran relaxed. "That's all I needed to hear." Gran nodded, giving Monica a wink. "Who's next on the board?"

"Hold on," I said. "Monica has to go on the board."

"Why?" Gran grumbled. "She didn't do it."

"And I believe her. But...what if someone is out to

frame her? Make her look guilty? We can't just leave her off because she's our friend. Sorry, Monica," I added, knowing what it was like to be a suspect.

She smiled thinly. "That's fine, I don't mind. The truth is ladies," she said, addressing Jenna and Gran, "I should be on the board. I was having a relationship with Llewellyn. I was with him the night he died."

"You were?" Gran and Jenna said in unison.

She nodded. "Yes."

"This is why Jackson isn't here." Jenna nodded. "Because the police haven't worked that out yet. Otherwise, you'd be down at the station."

"I'm going there after this," Monica told us. "I'd rather be seen as cooperating than hiding."

"I'll come with you," I offered, not wanting her to go on her own.

"Thanks."

Another boom of thunder rattled the walls and the lights flickered.

"Talk about dramatic flair." Whitney suddenly materialized, startling us all.

"Where have you been?" I asked, hand over my racing heart.

"What? Miss me?" she drawled, floating around the space in front of the murder board.

"Surprisingly, yes," I muttered.

"Awwww, you care," she cooed, smiling. Then her face dropped. "Actually, I've been hiding."

"Hiding?"

"Yeah. That demon hunter has been catching ghosts in his traps. I didn't want to get caught." She shivered, rubbing her hands up and down her arms.

I was already shaking my head. "No, he wasn't. I helped Llewellyn with his traps and they weren't for ghosts."

"They were. I saw it. With my own eyes," she protested.

"Saw what? Exactly?"

"Well." She floated up toward the ceiling. "I was taking a stroll along the Esplanade—I like to visit The Tea Leaf—so I was heading there when I saw that hunter guy pull up outside on his motorbike."

"Scooter," I corrected.

"Whatever." She waved away my interruption. "And he had one of those urn things with him."

I nodded. "That would be a trap, yes."

"So he took that inside The Tea Leaf. Naturally, my interest was piqued because I like to sit at one of their tables in the window and catch the afternoon sun. It's so quaint in there with their pink-and-white pinstriped wallpaper and roses on their teacups." She sighed, her face taking on a dreamy quality.

"What happened next?" Gran interrupted, saving me the trouble.

"Oh yes. So I followed, and the hunter guy was out

back with the urn and he placed it on a shelf in the storeroom."

"Were the Oliver sisters with him?" I asked.

Whitney nodded. "Yes, indeed. One of them looked really pissed off, like annoyed that they'd had to call him to deal with their problem, and the other one looked super happy he was there and kept lifting her hand to touch him when he wasn't looking."

Sounded about right. Poppy Oliver would have been the annoyed one. She struck me as an independent type. Between the two sisters, she was the one in charge. And I'd already seen how Hetty felt about Llewellyn—like most other red-blooded women in town, she idolized him. I could just see her getting in a sneaky touch.

"What were they talking about?" Jenna asked, head cocked to one side.

"Oh, I wasn't listening to them," Whitney protested. "That would be rude!"

Monica groaned. "What use are you then?"

"Well," Whitney grumbled, crossing her arms and frowning at Monica. "I hung around to see what the hunter fellow was trying to catch."

"And?" Monica's tone indicated she was getting annoyed with the ghost who refused to eavesdrop.

"It was a ghost!"

"A ghost of who?" I asked.

"Oh..." Whitney paused. "I hadn't thought of that. I don't know."

"What was this ghost doing?" I asked next. I remembered the Oliver sisters—Hetty—saying they had a poltergeist problem. Could that be the trap Llewellyn had set?

Whitney giggled. "Oh, it was a naughty ghost. He pulled out every single drawer in the kitchen and embedded all the utensils into the wall. I'm so glad no one was there at the time. They could have been hurt."

"Anything else?"

"He was always doing something naughty. Terrible, really," she admitted. "Threw all the food out of the fridge. Swiped everything off the shelves in the storeroom. But he was just a kid."

"A kid?" Jenna asked. "How old, do you think, this kid was?"

"Twelve or thirteen," Whitney said.

I looked at the others. "I'm pretty sure it was a poltergeist," I told them.

"A poltergeist?" Whitney gasped. Then... "What's that?"

"It's like a ghost gone bad," I explained. "They can move things around, throw things, destroy things. They can even hurt people."

"Oh. That explains it," she said.

"Explains what?"

"Well to begin with, when this kid ghost started coming around, Hetty and Poppy were pleased. They kept calling him Brigit, of all things, and just seemed really happy he was there. Of course, he didn't like being called Brigit, a girl's name. That's when he started acting out."

I met eyes with Jenna. "You think the Oliver sisters thought the ghost was someone else?" Jenna asked me.

I nodded. "I do. We should find out who Brigit was."

"Leave it with me." Jenna made a note on her phone.

Whitney continued. "They were really confused when he started trashing the place, kept asking Brigit what was wrong, only each time they called him that name he got angrier and angrier."

"Did something happen to make them call the demon hunter?" I asked.

Whitney nodded. "It sure did. He turned on the gas —to all of the burners. That place could have gone up in flames. Lucky neither of those ladies is a smoker because if they'd walked in in the morning with a lit cigarette. Boom!" Just as she said boom, a loud clap of thunder rattled the store and we all jumped.

"When was this?" I looked toward Monica and mouthed the words timeline. She nodded once in understanding and quickly taped together pieces of blank paper and taped them to the bottom of the murder board, moving so fast no one saw her do it. One minute the timeline wasn't there, the next it was.

"Well, the kid turned on the gas the night before last, so it was yesterday morning when the ladies called the hunter. He came out when they closed up shop last night. They didn't want him coming during opening hours, didn't want their customers to know they had trouble."

"I thought you said you didn't eavesdrop?" Gran pounced.

"Yes, well." Whitney sniffed. "I can't help but overhear things from time to time. It's not intentional."

"Thank you, Whitney—that's very helpful." I added Llewellyn's visit to The Tea Leaf to the timeline. Late afternoon yesterday was our starting point. Clearing my throat I glanced at Monica. "What time did you last see him?"

"He was in Brewed Awakening in the evening. Came in around eight. I threw him out around ten."

"Threw him out?"

She nodded. "He'd had a bit to drink and got into a bar fight. I tossed both their asses out."

"Who did he fight with?"

"That druid guy."

"Finn Hurley?" I couldn't have been more surprised. I hadn't laid eyes on Finn, or Morgan, since their arrival in Whitefall Cove and had pretty much written off any assistance they may have provided. To know that he was at the pub and fighting was unexpected.

"I guess. If that's the druid guy's name." Monica nodded. "Big guy. Broad shoulders. Tall." She indicated with her hands. "Not bad to look at either."

"Do you know what they were fighting about?"

"Llewellyn was all worked up and was calling him a fraud. That's all I know."

I already knew Llewellyn didn't trust Finn—or Morgan for that matter, but I had to admit I was surprised the two of them would physically fight. I sighed. If only Llewellyn were here to ask.

"You haven't seen Llewellyn—as a ghost—have you, Whitney?" It was a long shot.

She shook her head. "Told you. I was hiding from him. I thought he wanted to make me disappear."

I wondered if this was why the ghosts had been acting weird lately. Jackson had said they'd all disappeared on him. Was it because they were all afraid of the demon hunter? Although he'd assured me he wasn't here for the ghosts, what if he lied?

Whitney cleared her throat. "I may have seen where he went after he left Brewed Awakening though," she admitted.

"Say what now?" Monica's eyebrows rose. "You say you were scared of this guy, but you were following him around town? Girl, you're a stalker ghost, that's what you are!" Flipping her hair over one shoulder with disdain, Monica kept her dark eyes trained on Whitney. The rest of us swiveled our heads like we were watching a tennis match. Things were escalating unexpectedly—it was probably a good thing Whitney was already dead because the expression on Monica's face looked like she wanted to kill her. Which led me to believe she cared more about Llewellyn than she let on...why else would she act jealous that Whitney was following him around?

"Oh yeah?" Whitney shot back, hovering up near the ceiling as if to keep her distance. "Did he tell you he was visiting Vanessa Howe? Hmmm? Did he tell you that?"

All eyes back to Monica, who blanched. "What?" she squeaked.

Whitney nodded her head. "Mmmmhmmm. And he was naked!"

"You're a liar!" Monica shouted, jumping to her feet.

"Ladies, ladies!" I stepped between the ghost and the vampire. "Calm down. Monica." I drew her attention to me. "Vanessa was painting Llewellyn's portrait," I explained.

"His portrait?" she echoed.

I nodded. "Ummm, how do I put this..." I chewed my lip, sensing she wasn't going to take this next bit of news well.

"His nude portrait!" Whitney chortled, bursting into a fit of laughter, holding her stomach, doubled over with mirth, so much so she floated up through the ceiling.

"Was it?" Monica asked me, voice low. "A nude portrait?"

I nodded. "It was."

"Did he tell you?" I caught the hint of hurt in her voice that I knew something about him that she didn't.

I shook my head. "No. I stumbled upon it quite by accident," I reassured her. "He was...sitting...for her behind his RV."

"Were they..." She trailed off.

"She was behind her easel. Painting him." I didn't mention the fact that Vanessa had been wearing very little and the two of them were very comfortable around each other. Was Llewellyn sleeping with Vanessa? I couldn't say, but I silently wrote Vanessa's name on a Post-it and added it to the murder board. "When did you visit him?" I asked Monica, for it had to be after he'd seen Vanessa.

She huffed out a breath. "Just after one in the morning. Early closing on a weeknight. We shut up at midnight. I balanced the till, cleaned up, stopped home for a shower and change of clothes."

"And what time did you leave Llewellyn's place?"

"Around two thirty. He was sound asleep when I

left. I had things to do, couldn't afford to waste my night hours watching someone sleep."

"Fair enough." I added her information to the timeline and reluctantly placed a Post-it with her name on it on the murder board.

"That's it?" Gran asked, "That's all we got? Two suspects—both vampires? Nuh-uh, you've gotta broaden the net." Clambering out of her chair, she hurried over to me and snatched the marker out of my hand, scribbling on a Post-it. "First of all those Oliver sisters. You've got 'em on your timeline. They should be up here too." She stabbed a Post-it to the board. "And that druid bloke. Very suspect if you ask me." His name joined the Oliver sisters. Then she added one more.

"Morgan Healy?" I read. "Really? Why is she a suspect?" Morgan's name hadn't come up before now. I didn't figure how Gran considered her a suspect.

"Because stalker ghost here isn't the only one who sees what's going on in this town," Gran said somewhat triumphantly. Whitney hadn't reappeared after she'd drifted up through the ceiling and I figured something outside the store had caught her attention. Now that she was able to travel beyond the confines of my bookstore she'd started to venture out further and further.

"Night before last I saw Llewellyn Cox locking lips with Morgan Healy," Gran declared triumphantly.

You could have heard a pin drop. We all turned to look at Monica, who was fuming. Oh, this wasn't good, wasn't good at all. Monica moved so fast I couldn't track her movements, but the way the front door was swinging and the blast of cold air and rain told me that she'd left. I hoped it was to go and report in at the police station and not to confront Morgan.

CHAPTER
FOURTEEN

After Monica's sudden departure, we were subdued and called it a night. The storm still raged outside.

"Anyone need a lift?" I asked. "My car's out back."

"I'm good. I've got some stuff to take care of at work and my car's there anyway," Jenna said.

"You sure you don't want me to drop you off? I know it's just down the street, but the rain is coming down sideways out there," I offered.

She smiled. "I'll be fine. Is anyone going to go after Monica?"

I glanced at Gran who was already shaking her head. "No way. I'm not going near a pissed off vampire. No sir-re-bob."

"I'll check in on her. I don't think she'll do

161

anything stupid. Probably just needs to burn off some of that angst," I said.

"Did you know about her affair with Llewellyn?" Jenna asked, reaching for her umbrella.

I shook my head. "Not until today. She says it wasn't serious, but her reaction tonight when she learned that he didn't consider their relationship exclusive, I think that hurt her. And Monica has never been one to wear her heart on her sleeve. I expect she'll do whatever it is she does to blow off steam and then report in at the police station."

Jenna gave a curt nod. "Keep me posted." She opened the door and the wind snatched it from her fingers, slamming it back against the wall. "Holy heck." But Jenna was the determined type. Bracing herself, she stepped outside and opened her umbrella, which promptly turned inside out.

With a laugh I flung out my hand, encasing her in a weatherproof bubble. "Off you go," I shouted over the storm.

"Thanks!" She waved and hurried down the street, the wind helping her on her way. I stood just outside and watched, making sure she reached the *Tribune* offices safely, my own magic bubble keeping me warm and dry. Once Jenna had reached her destination, I closed and locked the door once more.

"Right, you guys," I addressed Gran and Archie. "Ready?"

"Yep." Gran leaned down and scooped Archie up from the chair. His head bumped her chin in delight.

Turning off the lights and setting the alarm, I led the way to the back door, stretched a protective bubble over the three of us, and hurried us all to my car.

"What do you know about Finn and Morgan?" I asked Gran after sliding behind the steering wheel.

Gran glanced at me. "Nothing much. Why?"

"I found out that they are working on repairing the rift to another dimension—that that is the source of our troubles, not non-existent wards."

Gran nodded. "I could have told you that." I bit back my annoyance that she hadn't. Gran could be...difficult...at times and right now I needed her to be cooperative, not belligerent.

"So you knew Izzy was lying? At the town meeting?"

She blinked rapidly. "I figured it was for the greater good." She was right of course. If Izzy had told the townsfolk exactly what was happening there would have been outright panic. Unfortunately, with Llewellyn's murder, we weren't far from that now.

"I'm curious why it's taking them so long...to fix the tear."

Gran swung her head to look at me. "Very good point, Harper love." She nodded. "With two experts on the case, you'd think they'd have had this settled within a matter of hours."

My point exactly. "Instead it's been days. And now you tell me that Morgan has been seeing Llewellyn? He told me he doesn't trust her—or Finn—at all. Out of all the people in Whitefall Cove I'd never expect Llewellyn to hook up with Morgan. Are you sure about what you saw?"

"Most definitely." Gran nodded vigorously. "I was dropping by his RV and she was coming out. He was standing in the doorway and she turned back, stood on the bottom step, reached up and pulled his head down for a kiss. A very long kiss. I expect it involved tongue."

"Too much information!" I protested.

"I wanted you to get a clear picture," Gran huffed. "This wasn't some chaste peck. It was a full-on kiss."

"Okay, okay, I get it." I pulled up out front of Gran's house, engine running. "Can you take Archie with you? I'm going to drop by the police station and if Monica's there I'll wait for her. It could be a long night and the weather is too foul for Archie to be out in it."

"Sure." Gran ruffled Archie's fur where he contentedly curled up on her lap. "Wanna have a sleepover, boy?"

"Mrew!" he answered. I waved my magic over them as Gran opened the door and Archie jumped out. She turned to say something, but the wind whipped her words away. A fork of lightning lit up the sky and I

couldn't help but wonder if this storm was due to the rift. It had rolled in fast and violent. I watched through the slapping windshield wipers as Gran and Archie hurried for her front door, my magic keeping them safe. Once they were inside, I dropped the protection and pulled away, dialing Jackson's number through the car's Bluetooth.

"Harper." He answered on the first ring.

"Are you at work?" I asked.

"I am." He paused. "Monica's here. I guess that's why you're calling."

"Partly. I'm coming in to offer moral support."

"Drive safe." We disconnected the call and I winced at how mundane we were. My feelings were still hurt that he'd left town abruptly without a word to me. To get past this we needed to sit down and talk it through, but that was hard to do when creatures from another world were invading your town and your best friend was a suspect in a murder. Plus it bothered me that I'd been solely focusing on my hurt feelings over Jackson's disappearance and not about Jackson himself. Was he okay? Something had happened, clearly, and a twinge of guilt at my selfishness had me squirming in my seat. We needed to talk about it, that much was clear.

Five minutes later I blew into the police station, the gust of wind at my back making me stagger.

Officer Lilliana Miles was behind the counter. Figures, since today had been such a shitty day. I didn't even make it to the counter. I was halfway when she pointed to a chair across the room and barked, "sit!"

I sat. I sat for a very long time. One hour. Then two. My stomach rumbled, reminding me I'd missed dinner and I glanced at my phone, checking the time. I knew Liliana had let Jackson know I was here; I'd overheard her not so dulcet tones. And I knew, given the tension in our relationship at the moment that he wouldn't have kept me waiting intentionally. Which meant he was busy interviewing Monica and it was taking a long time.

It was another hour before Monica appeared, Jackson behind her. Monica's face didn't give anything away, but then she'd always had the best poker face ever. Her eyes landed on me and she gave the slightest of nods. I stood, backside numb from sitting on the hard waiting room chair.

"All set?" I asked.

"Sure." Her eyes darted away and I saw it, a hint of vulnerability in her armor, a flash of fear in her eyes before she shut it down, freezing me out. I stepped forward and hugged her, felt her arms come around me and squeeze tight. This had rattled her. My fearless friend was afraid and my heart hurt for her.

"Remember," Jackson said, "no leaving town."

"Since when have I ever left this town, Detective?" Monica snapped, her usually friendly voice dripping in ice. "It's my home. I live here. There is no need for me to flee."

Jackson shuffled his feet and had the grace to look uncomfortable. "Yeah. Sorry," he said gruffly. "It's procedure."

She ignored him. "I'll wait in the car. Give you two a minute."

I sagged in relief that she wasn't ditching me. "Sure." I pointed my keys toward my car visible through the windows and unlocked it, the *beep, beep* inaudible over the sound of the storm.

Jackson and I watched as Monica strode out of the police station without a backward glance, then climbed into the passenger seat of my car. The sight of her sitting there, unmoving, statue-like was a little unnerving.

"She didn't do this," I said to Jackson, worry for my friend having my hands wringing together. Jackson stilled them with his.

"I hope for her sake that's true," he said solemnly.

"You can't believe she's guilty?" It was preposterous. Monica would never hurt anyone, ever. Just because she was a vampire did not make her a killer.

"This isn't the time or the place, Harper." Jackson

lowered his voice, jerking his head toward Liliana who was watching us with interest.

My hackles rose. "I would have thought this the perfect time and place," I argued. "You're the detective on Llewellyn's case. This is a murder investigation, this is a police station, and my best friend is a suspect."

He sighed, rested his hands on my shoulders and peered into my face. "You're angry with me. And you have every right to be."

Despite my self-lecture a couple of hours ago, he was right. I was seething mad and having him interrogate Monica had only exacerbated my already heightened emotions. A loud boom of thunder shook the building, and the night sky lit up with multiple lightning strikes. I clutched at Jackson's arms to keep my balance as the building rumbled and shook against the onslaught.

"This isn't normal," I muttered, peering out the window at the rain that continued to pour down and the unrelenting rumble of thunder.

"We're going to have flooding if the rain keeps up." Jackson frowned. "The storm drains won't be able to withstand this."

It clicked then. The storm. The foreboding feeling that had been dogging my heels for days. The sizzle and crackle of power in the air. Whoever was behind this, whatever they had planned, was happening tonight.

"What is it?" Cupping my chin, Jackson forced me to look at him, his voice concerned. "You've gone pale."

I jerked away. "I'm fine. Tell me, can you still see the dead?"

He inclined his head. "At times."

"Whitney told me the ghosts were hiding from Llewellyn, that they thought he was here to trap them," I told him. "Did any of them tell you the same?"

He shook his head. "They haven't been talking to me." He glanced outside. "You think this is related, don't you?"

I motioned for him to come closer and he did, ducking his head so his ear was close to my mouth. "I need to bring you up to speed with what I know and what's been happening in Whitefall Cove," I whispered. "But this is definitely not the place." My eyes shot to Liliana who was watching us with narrowed eyes, annoyance that she couldn't hear what we were saying evident by the way she frowned and leaned in our general direction.

"I'm done here. I'll follow you out to your place. I assume that's where you're taking Monica?" We both turned to look at my friend waiting in my car, only she wasn't. The passenger seat was empty.

"Monica!" I rushed for the door, concern for her overwhelming. As I rushed out into the storm the rain pelted at me, the wind joined in, buffeting me so hard I staggered. Shielding my eyes with my hands, I swept my glance up and down the street. She was gone. And I felt like an awful friend. I should have left immediately, not made her wait in the car.

"Harper!" Jackson shouted in my ear, catching hold of my arm and trying to drag me back into the police station, "Come inside. It's not safe out here."

Belatedly I summoned a bubble, encasing it around us both. Inside the bubble, there was no storm, just warm sweet air.

Jackson blinked in disbelief. "Oh."

I smirked. "Yeah, learned a few new tricks while you were away," I told him, no longer needing to shout to be heard.

"Harper—"

I cut him off. "I know. We need to talk. And we will. But not here. I'll meet you at the cottage."

"I'll be five minutes. Wait for me."

I shook my head. "I'll be fine. I can keep myself safe, Jackson, I don't need you for that." My words were harsher than I intended and he reared back as if I'd slapped him. Oh boy, did we have some repairing of our relationship to do. But beyond that, something very bad was about to happen in Whitefall Cove and I had to stop it.

"You do what you have to do. I'll see you at home." Reaching up, I gave him a peck on the cheek, then separated the magic bubble into two, taking one with me as I hurried around to the driver's side of my car and climbed inside.

Monica had left a note on the passenger seat. *Stop worrying, I'm fine. Love Mon xx.*

CHAPTER

FIFTEEN

The power was out by the time I got home. With a wave of my hand, the candles scattered around my cottage flared to life. It was odd being here without Archie—not only did I miss him but also I had a niggling fear I'd need him before the night was out. He was my familiar and, while I'd never used him to channel my power before, something told me tonight just may be that time.

Making a decision, I dialed Jackson—he could swing by and pick up Archie on his way here. Only, of course, the power was out, as was cell phone coverage. My stomach rumbled again, reminding me I hadn't eaten. I decided to eat while waiting for Jackson and then we could go pick up Archie together. It wouldn't hurt to check in on Gran. Rummaging in the fridge, I made myself a sandwich, poured myself a glass of wine and was sitting eating at the kitchen table when Jackson arrived.

"Geez!" He shook himself like a wet dog, water droplets flinging in every direction. "At least you won't flood up here. You've got the best position in the bay." He shrugged out of his raincoat and hung it over the back of a kitchen chair.

"Help yourself to a sandwich," I mumbled with my mouth full of ham and cheese. "Or wine."

"Still on duty. But thanks."

"'K." I continued eating, keeping my attention on my plate.

"Can I tell you what happened?" he asked.

"I don't know, can you?" My snark was unmistakable.

He sighed. "I meant, will you listen? I know you're pissed. I can see that. And I deserve it. I had good reason, Harper, but if you're not ready to hear what I have to say then I won't waste my breath saying it."

In other words, was I ready to stop being childish and cut him some slack?

Yes, I was. "Yes." I hated this tension between us and with a chill creeping up my spine I knew I needed to focus on what was to come. And I'd need my issues with Jackson resolved so I could concentrate on the battle ahead. For it was coming. It was inevitable. A crack of thunder punctuated the thought.

"You remember I told you about my partner, Bryan?"

"I do." I nodded. "You were both shot. He died. You didn't."

Jackson nodded. "Yeah well, he turned up that night at Brewed Awakening. And he was terrified."

"Of the demon hunter?"

But Jackson surprised me by shaking his head. "No. At first, he took me by surprise because I'd thought he'd crossed over already. He hung around for a long time in East Dondure while I was recovering. Keeping an eye on me and his wife I guess, making sure we were okay. And I promised him I'd look out for her."

"But not marry her as he wanted." I remembered Jackson telling me of his partner's request.

A small smile flittered across his face. "No. Never anything of a romantic nature. Anyway, Bryan appeared in Brewed Awakening shouting for my help. He was terrified."

"So you followed him." I nodded, remembering how Jackson had shot out of his chair and hot-footed it out of the bar.

"He was moving fast, gesturing for me to follow, so I did. I finally convinced him to stop and tell me what was going on. Before the shooting, we'd busted this drug ring, put away pretty much the entire gang, including the leader. Only last week they'd been moving prisoners after a fire in the jail and there'd been an attack on the bus they were in."

"A jailbreak?" I was shocked. I didn't think those things happened in real life.

Jackson nodded. "Two of the gang got away. Coincidently they were the leader and his second in command. The rest were recaptured within hours."

"You think it was a setup?"

"Could be. But this is what had Bryan rattled. They were coming for Samantha."

"His wife? Why?"

"Some stupid code. They couldn't take Bryan's life —he was already dead. So the next best thing is Sam."

"That's just stupid. She wasn't involved in any of it."

"You and I know that, but these guys have been behind bars for years and have spent that time dreaming up their revenge."

"Wait. Does that mean they were coming for you too?"

He nodded. "That was the plan. Take out Sam, head here for me."

"And they knew you were here?"

He rubbed his eyes. "I wasn't worried about me. I was worried about Sam. She's not a cop, she had no idea these guys had put a target on her back, and had no way to protect herself. I had to go. To protect her."

"Of course you did." No doubt about it. "Why didn't you tell me?"

"I should have. I'm sorry that I didn't." He dropped his head, studied his hands that sat loosely on the table. "My only excuse is that I was caught up in the moment—it was like I'd been transported back in time and the same fear and adrenaline rush of when Bryan and I were shot...just overwhelmed me. I hit the road immediately, I made calls to my old colleagues in East Dondure, put a plan in place. And in all of that was an overwhelming fear that if I didn't stop them, they'd not only kill Sam but that they'd come here next. For you."

"Me?" I reared back in surprise.

"What better way to hurt a cop than take away the one he loves the most—and leave him alive to suffer the loss."

"But you said the plan was they were coming for you."

"I was worried they'd change their minds on that one, I admit," he said sheepishly. "My fears may have been unwarranted. Paranoia had kicked in by this stage. Bryan was beside himself with worry over his wife and for the first time in my life, I knew how he felt. When it comes to you...I just don't think straight."

I blinked, taken aback. "I wish you'd told me." It all made perfect sense. Now.

"I wish I had too. I honestly don't know why I didn't. One part of me was thinking the less you knew the better, that if somehow they got here, got to you, you wouldn't be able to tell them anything, that it was better you didn't know."

"But if I were in danger, wouldn't it be fairer if I knew about it? So that I could take precautions?"

"That was the other argument I had with myself. And this argument went on for days. And then it was a moot point because we caught them and they are back behind bars." His laugh was self-deprecating. "And then I finally realized what an absolute mess I'd made of things. I'd ignored your calls because I didn't want you any more involved than I thought you were. Only it turns out you weren't involved at all—the gang had no idea you existed. Your danger was all in my imagination and I struggled to admit that I'd made such a colossal mess. And then it was too late. You were hurt and angry that I'd shut you down—as you should be—but I did it for the best of reasons. Because I love you. I love you so much it hurts and I thought I was protecting you. I'm sorry."

"Well." My head was spinning. As far as apologies went, his was pretty epic. "It's a good thing I love you too, Jackson Ward." I grinned, reaching across the table and placing my hand atop of his. His head snapped up, eyes zeroed in on mine, held my gaze. I nodded. It was true. I did love him, only those three little words were ones we'd never said to each other before.

We stood, leaned across the table, and kissed. Against my lips, he whispered, "I love you."

"I love you too," I breathed, before kissing him again. Long and hard. In perfect unison our breath hitched, our hearts beat in frantic synchronized rhythm, our hands wandered and sought out the other, held tight. All thoughts of the rift, the storm, Archie, all fled as I lost myself in Jackson's embrace. That is, until a loud clap of thunder shook the cottage, followed by the crashing noise of a tree branch coming through the kitchen window.

"Hell, it's bad out there." Jackson rushed to the kitchen to survey the damage. The branch hung half in and half out of my cottage. Edging closer to the window and peering into the blackness outside, Jackson shouted over the roar of the storm, "I can't tell if it's completely severed from the tree or not. I'm going to see if I can pull it inside. You go see what you can find to board up the window."

Grabbing his arm, I pulled him away from the window, broken shards of glass crunching underfoot. "No need," I yelled back. "I can fix this. Stand back."

Maneuvering myself in front of him I held out my hands. The massive branch trembled and slowly rose, then disappeared out the window. My arms started to shake with the effort and sweat dotted my brow.

"Well, I'll be damned," Jackson said, voice tinged with awe. "You can move things now?"

I nodded. "Llewellyn put me on to it, said he thought I was telekinetic. Turns out he was right." Giving my hands a shake, I held them out once more and concentrated all of my energy on the shards of glass on the floor. Moving the fallen branch was one thing. Could I fit all the shards of glass back into the windowpane, then merge them back together? The shards moved quickly, zipping from the floor to the broken windowpane and making a pinging noise as they fitted themselves into their respective spot. Sweat trickled down my spine, and my whole body trembled with the effort. Finally, the last piece of glass popped back into place, then the crushed remnants floated into the air, and smoothed over the window, filling in the tiniest of gaps until the window was whole once more.

"That was amazing!" Jackson slung his arm around my shoulders and I sagged against him, spent.

"It was exhausting," I admitted. With legs made of jelly, I made my way to a kitchen chair and plopped down into it.

"Can I get you anything?" He was hovering, concerned. It was sweet and I tried to smile to let him know I was okay, but I had a feeling it came across more like I was bearing my teeth than actually smiling. "That bad huh?" he said.

"Water?" I suggested. My wine glass was empty or I'd have slugged that down. Jackson busied himself getting me a glass of water while I closed my eyes and calmed my body. In my mind, I heard Llewellyn's voice: "You're a powerful witch. That little display is just a fraction of what you are truly capable of. You just need to believe." His voice began to fade away, echoing "believe" as it went. I did believe, I wanted to argue. Well, I was starting to believe, put it that way. So far everything Llewellyn had told me was true. I wished he were here so I could ask him more about the Whitelight Witch. My eyes popped open.

"Can we go to Llewellyn's RV?" I asked Jackson, who'd just returned with my glass of water. I took a grateful sip, my strength returning already.

"His RV? Why?"

"He mentioned that he thought I was the Whitelight Witch and I want to know more about it, who she is, if I may be her."

He frowned. "Who is the Whitelight Witch and why would he think that?"

"I don't know, that's why I want to check his RV, see if there's any info on her. She's part of the reason why he came to Whitefall Cove. He was on a mission to protect the Whitelight Witch. Catching demons while he was here was a bonus."

"This witch is telekinetic?"

I nodded. Jackson ran a hand through his hair, the strands standing on end. "Actually it wouldn't hurt to go and check the RV's secure. I'm betting no one thought to close up his greenhouse against this storm."

"You're right!" His poor plants would be copping an onslaught and even though Llewellyn wasn't here to worry about his greenhouse anymore, it still wasn't right that we stand back and let it be destroyed. "Let's go."

With my magic still replenishing, I nixed the idea of draining myself even further with a protective bubble. After all, this was just a storm, a little bit of rain never hurt anyone. Bundling into my raincoat, I followed Jackson out to his car, the rain relentless, the wind doing its best to prevent our progress. All the while I had the sense something else was here. Something was watching us.

Climbing into the passenger seat, I slammed the door, peered through the water running down the glass. Through the darkness I saw a flash of red, like demons' eyes.

"Hurry." I urged Jackson. He didn't need much urging, turning the key in the ignition and peeling away with all four tires spinning as we fishtailed down the road.

"You saw it?" I asked, gasping and clutching the dash.

"I saw it," he replied, voice grim. We were running out of time. If we were to save Whitefall Cove from being annihilated by creatures from the other side, we had to do it tonight.

CHAPTER
SIXTEEN

Llewellyn's greenhouse was in a bad way. Pots were smashed on the floor, soil and plants unearthed and lying in puddles. The wind had wreaked havoc. Jackson unhooked the propped-open windows from the outside while I secured them from the inside. I was standing amongst the chaos when I spotted it, still dangling from its hook. The magic cauldron. Lifting it down, I clutched it to my chest and made my way out of the greenhouse, sending up a promise to Llewellyn that I'd come back, preferably with Jenna who was a gardening genius, and sort out his greenhouse.

"Did Llewellyn have a will?" I shouted as we trudged toward the RV. Jackson had a key and unlocked the door and I gave him a surprised look as I clambered inside. Once he followed me in and slammed the door I lit the candles. It was strange in the RV. The way the wind buffeted it made it feel like we were in motion, moving along the open road. Not that I'd traveled in an RV before—it was just how I'd imagined it would be.

"No will has turned up yet," Jackson said, shaking the rain off.

"So what happens to all of this?"

"The state will sort it out. They'll track down any relatives he may have." A vicious gust shook the van and I staggered, keeping hold of the cauldron with one hand while clutching the sink with the other.

"Right. It's not safe here," Jackson said. "With this wind, the whole RV could tip over. What was it you were looking for? Let's find it and get out of here."

"You'd let me take evidence?" I blinked in surprise. For some reason, I'd thought Jackson would insist that nothing leave the RV.

"I'd be taking it. You just happen to be with me." He looked at me, eyes zeroing in where I clutched the cauldron. "And whatever object it is that you're hugging."

"You can't see it?" Llewellyn had said the cauldron was magic, but again, I'd only half-believed him.

Jackson shook his head. "A bucket perhaps? Something round."

"It's a cauldron. Llewellyn's magic cauldron to be precise, and only he could see it. Except I could too. It was hanging in the greenhouse and...I don't know. Instinct told me to take it, so I did." I bit my lip, hoping I wasn't about to get in trouble with the law.

Jackson lifted one shoulder in a half shrug. "I can't even see it, so no harm, no foul. Although I'd suggest if it's got a handle, that you carry it by that. Avoid looking like you've got some sort of deformed arm injury."

I grinned and set the cauldron on the sink. Dusting my hands together, I glanced around. "So Llewellyn told me he was a hunter, a gypsy, and a mystic."

"Right?" Jackson followed my gaze around the RV. "So what?"

"So all of those things mean he's got to have a stash of books somewhere. Ancient tomes, folklore and the like." I started opening cupboard doors, peering inside. Jackson did the same.

"Whoa." He stood back, the small closet doors stood open, and I peered around him to see what was inside. There had been a fake back in the closet and behind it, weapons—of the demon-hunting variety.

"Makes sense," Jackson said more to himself than to me. Pulling out the clothes, he tossed them on the bed, then eyeballed the floor of the closet. Pulling out a pocket knife he wedged it into the side and sure enough, the whole thing lifted, revealing a hidden cavity beneath it.

"I hate to say it, but your fellow officers did a crap job of searching this place," I pointed out.

He glanced at me, brows drawn in a frown. "You're not wrong." Reaching in, he pulled out a small wooden chest and passed it to me. It was heavy and I heaved it onto the bed before flicking open the locks and opening the lid. Eureka! Books. Old, worn, leather-covered books.

I shut the lid and snapped the locks closed. "I'll take it with me," I said. Jackson was stuffing a pillowcase with the wooden and steel weapons hanging in the back of the closet. Swords, axes, crossbows. All old and from the look of them, homemade.

"Too dangerous to leave these here." He grunted under the weight of his haul. "The last thing we need is some idiot getting their hands on them and injuring themselves." He glanced at me. "Ready?"

"Yup." I looped my arm through the handle of the cauldron so it dangled from my elbow and although the weight of it jarred my shoulder I gritted my teeth and pressed on. We only had to get as far as the car parked outside. Hefting the wooden chest into my arms, I ground out. "Let's go."

Jackson led the way, the wind snatching the door out of his hands and slamming it against the side of the RV. He disappeared into the night and I followed, head down against the elements, practically colliding with Jackson at the back of his SUV. He tossed the weapons in the back and turned to take the chest from me, placing it in the back before slamming the door shut. "Get in!"

We drove to Gran's, the cauldron on my lap, the chest and weapons bouncing around in the back. Despite the torrential rain, Jackson drove fast and I was thankful for my seatbelt holding me in place. Within no time at all, he screeched to a halt out in front of Gran's. Another battle with the weather as we retrieved our haul from the back of the RV and struggled to Gran's front door. Jackson pounded on it with his fist, his body up close behind me and providing a buffeting shelter from the storm. Gran flung open the door and ushered us inside.

"Have you strengthened your wards today?" I grunted, turning into the living room and dumping the wooden chest onto the coffee table. I set the cauldron on the floor by an armchair where no one would trip over it.

"I doubled down." She nodded, hands-on-hips, covered from head to toe in a panda onesie.

"Nice onesie," Jackson said, dropping the stash of weapons by the front door. Now that we'd found them, he was loath to let them out of his sight. He caught me looking at them and said, "One of these could potentially be the murder weapon."

My mouth dropped open. I hadn't considered that.

And then a second thought. "You don't think it was Monica?"

He shook his head. "Preliminary findings are in from the coroner. The puncture wounds are too precise to be fangs. Fangs, like any other tooth, are not exactly the same and they are not circular. They leave more of an oval puncture wound and the very nature of biting someone would result in tearing, to some degree, of the skin. The two puncture holes on Llewellyn's wrist were most certainly made by some sort of instrument. I was leaning toward medical, but now that I've found these..." He nodded toward the weapons. "With all the spikes and blades in that lot, we might just have a match."

I punched his shoulder. Hard.

"Hey!" he protested, rubbing where I hit him. "What was that for?"

"You let me think Monica was a suspect. At the police station."

"Yeah well, I could hardly tell you the truth there, could I? With Liliana watching us and ready to report me the second I screwed up."

"She'd do that?" I knew she disliked me and I could live with that, but I didn't think she'd mess with Jackson's career, not out of spite.

He ran a hand around the back of his neck, the gesture showing how very weary he was. "She's been on edge, like everyone else in town. To be seen divulging particulars of the case—especially to a civilian—might be enough to tip her over the edge. But I've told you now, so..."

I decided to let him off the hook because he was right. He was a cop. I wasn't. He couldn't be seen telling me about an active case, especially in the police station of all places.

"But I was right, wasn't I, that his blood had been drained?" I remembered the grey color of Llewellyn's skin and the lack of blood around the wounds on his wrist. "Is that why his wrist was slashed as well, do you think? That the killer used one of his weapons to make the puncture holes, but the blood wasn't draining fast enough, so they slit his wrist?" I shuddered at the thought.

"That's the theory I'm working on," he confirmed.

I sank onto the sofa and Jackson sat next to me, putting a comforting arm around my shoulders. Gran was already rummaging in the wooden chest, lifting out the various books and parchments inside. "The question is," she said, "who would want his blood? And for what purpose?"

"Both excellent questions." Jackson nodded.

I longed for my murder board where I could track all of this. And suddenly, by merely thinking about it, it appeared. Gran shrieked and dropped the book she was holding, leaped backward and onto the armchair as if the biggest spider in the world had just crawled across her foot. It hadn't. But Gran wasn't aware of my telekinetic abilities and, to be honest, I didn't have much of a clue what I was doing with them either.

"Wraow mew mraw maow?" Archie appeared in the doorway, saw me, and quickly made his way over, jumping onto my lap and rubbing my chin.

"Yeah, I agree," I told him, stroking my hand along his fur. "I missed you too."

"What"—Gran pointed at the murder board that was suspended in the air in front of the fireplace—"is that?!"

I grinned. It was fun catching her unawares for a change. "It's the murder board, Gran."

"Yes, I can see that, Harper," she growled. "What is it doing here? In my living room?"

"I brought it here." I blinked, eyes wide. "Didn't I tell you? I'm telekinetic now."

She looked from the murder board to me and back again. "Well, I'll be damned!" She plopped down from her crouched position onto her backside. "You are a Whitelight Witch."

"Llewellyn told you?" It didn't surprise me. Gran had a way of getting people to spill their secrets—not that Llewellyn's hunch that I was the Whitelight Witch was a secret. He'd probably handed over that little nugget of info straight away.

She nodded. I pointed to the books spread out

across the coffee table. "I was hoping to find out more info in his books."

Gran surprised me by saying, "Oh, I can tell you about the Whitelight Witches. They're rare. You're rare," Gran amended, switching her attention to me.

"Wait. *They're* rare? There's more than one?"

She waved her hand in dismissal. "Of course. Like humans have different races yet they are all human, so it is with witches. There are different kinds. But don't get caught up on that. Being a Whitelight Witch is just a name. You're not going to start shooting white light out of your palms or anything." I sagged a little in relief. I had wondered if that was going to happen. "It just means your magic is based on the energy of a star —rather than the earth."

"A star?"

"Yeah...you know, stars twinkle at night? White lights in the sky?" she prompted.

"Oh!" I got it. "What star?"

"Now, that I don't know."

"And this star's energy, it's what feeds my magic? And that's why everyone has been telling me what a powerful witch I am? Because I'm not channeling my magic from the earth at all but from the universe?"

Gran puffed out a breath, but nodded. "I'm sure there's probably more to it, but yes. To be honest I never thought Whitelight Witches were real—they're almost like a genetic anomaly—but when Llewellyn started spouting that he thought you were one, well, I had to admit I had to adjust my thinking — and admit that he just might be right."

"Wait." Jackson interrupted with a hand on my knee. "Llewellyn was telling anyone and everyone that he thought Harper was a Whitelight Witch?"

Gran cocked her head. "Dunno. I don't think he was keeping it a secret."

"I don't think he was telling people." I patted Jackson's hand where it gripped my knee. "We'd talked about it; he was aware of the danger. He wouldn't have been that careless." I could guess why Jackson was concerned. He was worried that whoever was behind the trouble in Whitefall Cove—and Llewellyn's murder—would want to try and harness my magic. To distract him I nodded to the murder board hovering in front of us. Funny how holding it there took no effort, it was as natural to me as breathing. I wished Llewellyn were here to see it.

"Let's focus on this, and what we know."

"Before we get started..." Gran jumped up from her seat. "How about hot toddies?" Before we could answer she'd shuffled out, her panda tail wriggling on her butt.

CHAPTER
SEVENTEEN

The lights flickered, flickered again, and then stayed on.

"Power's back," Jackson commented, nursing the hot toddy Gran had made. The drinks were potent, of course. I'd only had a sip of mine, but Jackson was halfway done and was already feeling the buzz of triple shot whiskey judging by the glazed look in his eyes.

"Lemme get this straight." Gran squinted at the murder board where I'd been adding notes. "Llewellyn arrives in Whitefall Cove searching for the Whitelight Witch, but dark magic dulls his vision so he's not getting a clear picture of who she is? Then he starts a casual relationship with Monica, booze, weed, sex... " Gran sighed wistfully. "Lucky girl! He's also posing for a nude portrait for Vanessa Howe, he got into an argument with Finn Hurley, and has been sucking face with Morgan Healy. Oh, and he's supplied the Oliver sisters with a butt load of herbs for their tea shop. And he's been teaching you magic and how to set demon traps. Have I covered everything?"

Nodding, I chewed on my lip as I examined the board. Llewellyn certainly got around.

"What were Llewellyn and Finn fighting about?" I asked no one in particular. We'd seen very little of the druid or the sorceress since they'd arrived in Whitefall Cove. Izzy had called them in to help, but from what I'd seen they'd done very little. It had been Llewellyn who'd been running all over town setting traps and dealing with the creatures coming in through the rift.

"All Monica said was that she overheard Llewellyn call him a fraud," Jackson said, eyeballing his hot toddy and setting it down on the coffee table unfinished. I grinned. That was probably a wise move. Gran could drink him under the table any day of the week.

"Has anyone noticed how similar Finn and Morgan's surnames are?" Gran asked. "Hurley and Healy."

"I'm not sure that's relevant." They were similar, yes, but that didn't mean it was suspicious. Plus Finn was a druid and Morgan a sorceress, he was from the Otherworld, she was from Earth. At least I assumed she was. "How much do we know about Finn and Morgan?"

"Not much," Jackson said.

"Other than their names and that they're both insanely good looking? Nothing." Gran said.

"But you saw Llewellyn kissing Morgan, yes?"

Gran nodded. "I did."

I turned to Jackson. "Is it too late to visit them? We need to know what Finn was arguing with Llewellyn about and we need to know the extent of Llewellyn's relationship with Morgan—what if they were a couple and she thought it was serious and then discovers he's been sleeping with Monica?"

"We're not going anywhere tonight," Jackson said. "Not in this storm. And I can't take you with me on official police business," he added.

"Oh." I slumped in disappointment. But he was right, although the power was back on, and the storm sounded like it had eased up a little, it was still a wild and wooly night outside. Plus there was a demon with red eyes stalking me. I'd caught another glimpse of it when we'd left Llewellyn's RV. Other than its eerie red eyes I hadn't managed to make out the rest of it, which made it all the scarier. Jackson was right. We could wait until daylight. I already knew as soon as he left for work I'd find a way to talk to the supernatural duo on my own.

Gran picked up Jackson's hot toddy and pushed it

into his hand. "If you're staying you may as well drink this and not waste it." She picked up her empty cup and stood. "Another?" she asked me.

My cup was still full. I'd only had one sip. "I'm good, thanks, Gran. You go ahead."

Jackson did as he was told and drained the contents of his mug, then settled back on the cushions of the sofa. Before long his eyes drooped. Archie was spread out in front of the fireplace, toasting his belly in front of the flames. The crackle of the fire and the dim rumble of thunder was somewhat soothing. My lids were starting to feel heavy, but I wanted to go through Llewellyn's books before turning in for the night. It was a given that we were staying at Gran's. For one, it meant I wouldn't worry about her being here alone, and two, her knowledge of everyone and everything in town could come in handy.

I woke in the morning with Archie sprawled across my face. Spitting out cat fur, I pushed him off.

"Maow mrur," he protested before stretching and heading out the door. I was stretched out on Gran's sofa. Alone. Sitting up, I glanced around. No sign of Jackson. He'd fallen asleep early last night. I'd thrown a blanket over him before moving to sit on the floor by the fire and go through Llewellyn's books. Eventually,

my eyes had grown so heavy I'd had to give up and I'd snuggled up next to Jackson on the sofa, smiling when he'd wrapped an arm around my waist in his sleep and tugged me close, preventing me from falling off. That was the last thing I remember.

"Oh good, you're awake." Gran breezed in, swept up the cups from last night, and breezed out again. I screwed up my eyes at the sight of her in her transparent negligee.

"Clothes, Gran!" I shouted at her retreating back. I heard her muttering in the kitchen, wondering what she'd done to deserve such a prudish granddaughter. Pushing myself to my feet, I shuffled to the bathroom, splashed water on my face and smoothed down my hair as best I could.

"Hungry?" Gran asked when I appeared in the kitchen. "I've got pancakes or bacon and eggs. Or both." She had set her magic to work cooking up a feast.

"Pancakes would be great." I slid it into my usual chair at the table, a pang of homesickness overtaking me. I'd missed this. Sitting with Gran in her kitchen while she prepared a meal—or more correctly, her magic prepared a meal.

"Did Jackson leave already?" I asked, stifling a yawn. Seeing the coffee pot was full, I used my magic to pour myself a cup and levitate it across the room to the kitchen table.

"Mmmhmm." Gran nodded. She'd thrown a fluffy purple dressing gown over the flimsy negligee, thank goodness. "You were out cold. Must've been tired, love."

"Yeah, haven't been getting much sleep lately," I admitted, although I was surprised I hadn't woken when Jackson left. He must've climbed over me to get off the sofa. It was amazing he hadn't disturbed me.

"You are looking a bit haggard," she agreed. I grimaced. Gran wasn't one to mince her words; she pretty much told it like it was...whether you wanted to hear it or not.

"About this Whitelight Witch business." I changed the subject.

"What about it?" Her back was to me while she supervised the cooking of breakfast.

"I don't get how I can be a Whitelight Witch. I mean, genetically. Mom and you are both earth witches. How is it even possible that I draw my magic from the stars?"

Gran glanced at me over her shoulder, "No clue, love. It is what it is."

I was pondering my origins when it came to me. A brilliant idea. "I've got it," I said with a snap of my fingers.

"It better not be catching," Gran retorted and I snorted.

"No," I told her, "a cover for interrogating Finn and Morgan."

"Interrogating?" Gran cackled. "Listen to you."

"Okay, okay, talking to them. They must know about the Whitelight Witches, surely?"

Gran nodded, sent a plate full of pancakes flying through the air in my direction. I caught the plate and put it down in front of me with a frown.

"What? They not to your liking?"

"No...it's just that...you flew them through the air..."

"Yeah? So?"

"So you must be telekinetic too." Now that I thought about it, my telekinesis wasn't such a rare and new thing at all—the magic I'd been using all along involved moving objects through the air.

Gran shook her head and carried her own plate of bacon, eggs, fried tomato and mushrooms to the table. "Nope. You're confusing telekinesis with air magic."

"What's the difference?"

"Air magic is smaller and often tied to another spell. For example, the pancakes floating across the room? That's part of my cooking spell. If I were sitting in the living room and wanted something brought to me? That would be telekinesis. For one, it's further away, and two, I can't see it. They're not big distinctions, but they do make a difference."

"Oh."

"You sound disappointed," she observed, mouth full of food.

I chewed the inside of my cheek. Not disappointed, more that I didn't want to be the odd one out. I didn't want to be different. I was already weary of being told I was a powerful witch—it was almost like I didn't want that responsibility—especially since I'd never truly embraced my witch heritage. To be constantly told you're powerful, you're special, you're different...it came with expectations. Ones I wasn't sure I could fulfill. Add to that the whole Whitelight Witch thing and my magic coming from the stars? I was starting to feel more like a freak show than ever.

Gran smiled and patted my hand. "It'll all work out, love. Don't stress." I returned her smile, but worry continued to niggle away at me. What would our coven think of this? It had to change the dynamics, surely, and in all honesty, it was another change that right now I didn't want to face.

Gran interrupted my internal musings to ask, "What's the plan for today?"

I made a popping noise with my lips while I considered my plans. "Wendy is taking care of the store today. I think I'll head straight to Drixworths to talk with Finn and Morgan. Then I need to go and check Llewellyn's traps and reset them." I still harbored a sense of urgency that something bad was going to happen. It had been with me constantly for days. Probably why I looked so haggard, as Gran put it.

She was nodding now, poked her fork at me. "Good plan. I'm coming too."

"Sure," I agreed, caught her surprised expression, and guessed she'd been expecting me to argue. But the truth was, I was worried. And I wanted to keep Gran close, keep her safe. I knew she had her magic to protect herself with, but still...

"You're really rattled," she observed now, eyes shrewd. I rolled my shoulders. It sounded stupid when I said I had a feeling, for that's all it was. Outside of the red-eyed beast that had been stalking me, that is. I second-guessed myself, wondering if Gran might be safer staying far away from me.

"It's exhausting watching you think." Gran groaned, finishing breakfast and sending her plate to the sink where it began to wash itself. "I'm going to shower and get dressed. Do not leave without me."

She pinned me with her sharp eyes and I chuckled, holding up my hands. "I won't, I promise."

While Gran got ready, I finished breakfast, had another coffee, fed Archie from the stash of kibble Gran kept on hand for him, then meandered back into the living room. I noticed the pillowcase full of weapons was gone, but the wooden chest with Llewellyn's books was still sitting on the coffee table. They hadn't revealed much. A lot of botanical tomes, a couple of mythology books on demons and weapons required to defeat them, a personal journal that only had a couple of entries and, given Llewellyn's colorful lifestyle, were rather dull. Plus a notebook with an inventory of sorts of his greenhouse.

"Ready," Gran singsonged from the staircase. I wandered into the hallway to check out what today's fashion choice was. She didn't disappoint. A go-go dancer outfit, complete with psychedelic patterns and bright colors, white knee-high Ugg boots, and a matching headband. Massive white hoops adorned her ears, and neon blue eyeshadow finished the look.

"The seventies called," I teased.

"I know, I look great, right?" She sashayed her way down the staircase to meet me at the bottom.

"You look awesome as always, Gran."

It wasn't until we'd stepped out of the front door that I remembered my car was still at my cottage. We'd come here last night in Jackson's. Which meant....

"I'm driving!" Gran practically clicked her heels together in glee. I rolled my eyes. Gran approached driving the same way she did everything else, with great gusto and enthusiasm but perhaps not quite enough attention to detail. I was amazed she still held a driver's license, considering the number of infringement notices she'd racked up over the years. Gran had a motto that she'd park wherever she wanted, whenever she wanted, and no sign was going to change that.

Her Volkswagen bug was just like Gran—a one of a kind. It was candy apple red with large yellow flowers. I guess with such a distinctive car the locals could see her coming and knew to get out of her way.

CHAPTER
EIGHTEEN

Drixworths was thankfully calm this visit. Archie trotted behind me as we pushed through the massive doors. The witch with the purple hair who I'd helped battle the gremlin with passed by, spotted us and stopped. "Alice Brewer? Is that you?"

"Hey, Dulcie." Gran waved. "Long time no see." Within seconds the two witches had their heads together and were cackling away.

Figuring Gran would be safe enough under Drixworths roof, I made my way to the rear of the building, intent on getting to the basement without Izzy knowing I was here. If there was one thing I'd learned from Gran it was that it was easier to ask forgiveness than permission and my feelings were still hurt that Izzy had lied to me. To the entire town. And I instinctively knew she'd try and stop me from speaking to Finn and Morgan.

Behind the grand staircase was the door to the basement. Glancing around to make sure the coast was clear, I turned the knob and the door swung open. Archie darted in ahead of me and I followed, quietly closing the door behind me. Down the narrow staircase we went, magic lamps adorning the brick walls and casting enough light to see by. I could hear the murmur of voices, muffled, but the further we descended the clearer they became. Finn and Morgan. Discussing what? I couldn't quite make it out and I didn't want to start off on the wrong foot by loitering on the staircase and eavesdropping—although it was very tempting to do just that. I needn't have worried though, Archie announced our arrival by trotting ahead of me and drawing their attention, so by the time I reached the bottom of the stairs they were waiting.

"Hi!" I smiled as if this were an everyday occurrence.

"How did you get in?" Finn asked, hands on his hips.

I cocked my thumb behind me. "Errr. The door. At the top of the stairs."

"That door is locked." Morgan sneered, tossing her head, her white hair cascading down her back.

I shook my head. "It isn't."

"It is."

I bit my tongue. "Look, we could be here all day arguing if the door was locked or unlocked. Obviously, I'm here." I waved a hand up and down in front of myself. "So there's no point in arguing over it."

Finn shot a frustrated glare at Morgan. "It's what she does," he said. "Argue. About every little thing." Then he moved and I got a glimpse of what his big body had been blocking. A slowly spinning, hoop-like, glowing apparition, made up of streams of light going around and around in a rainbow of colors.

"Mrew?" Archie sat at my feet and watched the apparition.

"Don't get any closer," I whispered, not wanting him to get sucked into whatever that thing was.

"What's that?" I asked Finn, deciding he was the more approachable of the two.

"None of your business," Morgan snapped, her hands clenched into fists. Why was she so aggressive?

"She's pissed off you got in here," Finn answered my unspoken question, shooting her a glare. My gaze traveled between the two of them. It was impossible to miss the hostility in the air, so thick you could cut it with a knife. Again, I wondered why. And was this why the rift remained open? Because these two couldn't stop bickering long enough to work together?

"What can we do for you, Harper?" Finn asked,

arms folded over his chest, head cocked to one side as he waited for my reply.

I cleared my throat. "I was wondering what you knew about Whitelight Witches," I said. There was a beat, a shimmer in the air, almost as if the atmosphere itself had sucked in a breath. Then all was normal again.

"Oh great, she knows!" Morgan threw her arms up in the air dramatically and spun away as if me knowing I was a Whitelight Witch was the worst thing in the world.

"Could you cut the theatrics for one damn minute?" Finn snapped.

"Why? Wasn't I meant to know?" I was so confused.

Finn sighed, running his hand around the back of his neck. "We sensed you as soon as we arrived," he told me. "Only it was apparent you weren't aware so it was agreed it wasn't our place to interfere."

I narrowed my eyes. "Who agreed? The two of you? Or was Izzy involved too?"

Morgan and Finn exchanged a look, then Morgan shrugged. "She didn't think you were ready."

I stood looking at them, fury burning through my veins. How dare they? How dare she? My fingers curled and I felt my magic dance along my knuckles.

"Mreow." Archie rubbed against my leg, reminding me of why we were here. And possibly to calm down.

But I was finding it hard to keep control of my emotions. If anything, they felt amplified and, despite sucking in a breath and trying to slow my madly beating heart, a shot of electricity shot from my hand towards the slowly spinning hoop.

"Mreet, rowr, rowr." Archie stood on his hind legs and pawed at my thigh. I scooped him up, clutching him to my chest, my face buried in his fur. I felt it then, his calming presence wrapping around me, like a cozy warm blanket on a cold day. A shuddering sigh shook my body before I got a hold of myself— and my magic—and raised my head to eye Finn and Morgan.

"What is going on here?" I ground out, eyeing them and the strange hoop apparition with distrustful eyes. The energy was off in the basement and they were behind it. Them and the shining hoola hoop currently spinning its merry little dance in the middle of the room.

"Nothing," Morgan lied. Like Izzy, I could taste her lie in the air, bitter. Finn didn't say a word. I wasn't sure what was better, being lied to or being ignored.

I gasped. "It's you!" Oh my God, why hadn't I realized it before? It made perfect sense. "You created the rift." They didn't flinch at my accusation, nor protest their innocence. Then I had a second, cautionary thought. Maybe I should have kept my mouth shut. Like it or not, these two were powerful individuals and could probably toast my butt, even if I was plenty powerful in my own right.

Finn and Morgan looked at each other in silence and I swallowed. Oh dear. I was mentally calculating how fast I could get up the stairs when they burst out laughing. I almost sagged in relief. But I didn't put Archie down, just in case I still needed to make a hasty retreat. Instead, I waited for them to get their mirth under control, which took longer than I would have liked. Honestly, they were like a couple of kids. Morgan would finally get herself under control, look over at Finn, then burst into another fit of giggles, clutching her stomach with tears running down her face.

"Seriously?" I muttered. "It's not that funny."

Finn sobered, ground his knuckles into his eyes to wipe away the moisture. "Sorry, sorry." He coughed, wiped a hand over his face, slowly sobering. "You were saying?"

I pointed to the hoop. "What. Is. That?" I enunciated slowly and clearly.

"Well, you are right in one way," Finn said. Morgan had retreated to the other side of the room, her back to us. From here it looked like she was wiping her face, probably cleaning up the smeared makeup. "That is a portal."

"To?"

"The Otherworld."

"Oh." The Otherworld. Finn's home dimension. "So it's open all the time?"

"It's not really open. Think of it as a doorway. At the moment the doorway is here, unlocked, waiting to be opened. I only open the door when I want to pass through. But I have to keep the portal active to a certain degree so I can get back home when I'm ready."

Drat. A perfectly reasonable explanation. I narrowed my eyes. "Why were you fighting with Llewellyn then?"

Finn snorted. "That brat? Little upstart was accusing me of what you just did." He rubbed a hand over his chin. "Hmmm, I wonder if he caught a peek at the portal and jumped to the same conclusion you did. Wouldn't put it past him to break in."

"Well, if you are the real deal, why isn't the rift closed? Or repaired? Or whatever needs to happen to stop the invasion of other dimension beasties?" I demanded.

"We're working on it." Morgan was back, makeup immaculate, frosty attitude in place.

"Were you having an affair with Llewellyn Cox?" I asked her, changing the subject. Finn had satisfactorily answered my questions and now it was her turn.

"What?" they said in unison, only Morgan's voice was six octaves higher than usual.

At her squeaky response, Finn's eyebrows shot into

his hairline and he looked at her incredulously. "You and Cox were getting it on?" he asked, lips twitching.

She studied her nails. They were painted white and filed into points. Combined with the tribal tattoos on the back of her hands she looked totally badass. "I was not having an affair with him." She didn't meet my eyes. Or Finn's.

"Have you, at any time in the past, had a romantic relationship with him?" I pressed. The devil was in the details.

She blanched, eyes ricocheting away from me and Finn, looking anywhere but at us.

Finn's mouth dropped open. "You did!" He pointed a finger at her, then began laughing. "Oh my God. You used to have the hots for Cox." He laughed harder than he had when I accused them of opening the rift. Morgan crossed her arms and waited while I looked on. Things were getting interesting now. Even Archie was entranced.

"So?" Morgan drawled, clearly trying not to let him see how affected she was. I cocked my head, watching her. Was she upset Llewellyn was dead? Hard to say. Morgan wore her magic like a shield, keeping her emotions invisible. She looked like butter wouldn't melt in her mouth, but I wondered if she was hurting on the inside.

I cleared my throat, drawing her attention. "Okay, so we can safely say that you and Llewellyn were an item at one time," I said, "and I'm sure the police will be talking to you about this soon so I may as well give you the heads up that a witness saw you...leaving his RV."

"Leaving his..." Finn hooted with laughter, holding his belly and leaning over so far I feared he'd fall flat on his face.

Morgan stood ramrod straight, her eyes drilling into me. "A witness?"

"Mmmhmm. We know the two of you shared a kiss."

A muffled snort came from Finn. "This keeps getting better and better."

"Enough!" Morgan shouted, startling me. "Get out!" She pointed to the staircase, her eyes blazing with anger.

"Hey now." Finn sobered and straightened up, approaching Morgan who had her hand raised as if debating whether to launch an attack—or not.

"You shut up," Morgan snapped, flicking a finger at him. A blast of magic hit him in the chest, but rather than recoil, it simply bounced off. I swallowed. Yep. Powerful. I didn't think it was wise to get in the middle of the two of them if they were going to square off. I also didn't want her to turn the attack on me.

"Don't tell me..." Finn paused and peered at her, then stepped closer, into her personal space. I thought she'd explode but instead, she sort of deflated. "Oh shit." Finn tugged her toward him, wrapping her in his big arms and cradling her against his chest. "You friggin cared for the little weed." He rolled his eyes as he patted her back.

Archie began to purr and I almost burst out laughing. Okay. This had not panned out the way I expected, but I didn't want to leave without all the answers, and I still had one question unanswered.

"Go ahead." Finn sighed, watching me over Morgan's head. I wasn't sure if she was crying or merely leaning on him, but given that she projected such an ice queen image, I was reasonably confident she had no intention of looking up until I left.

"Everyone's a mind reader these days," I grumbled.

Finn smiled. "Ever been told you're an open book?" he teased.

"Yes. Frequently."

"Well then." He smirked, one eyebrow raised.

"Okay, look. Why is repairing the rift taking so long? You two are powerful, I can feel it. I just don't understand what the hold up is."

He sighed. "The problem is, whoever opened it is working to keep it open. And we haven't been able to pinpoint their location, so we've been unable to block their signal, so to speak."

"So the rift *was* intentional?"

Finn nodded, face grim. "And now I suggest you

leave because this one is coming out of her stupor and she will not be pleased to discover you're still here."

I didn't need telling twice. I shot up the staircase, called down a hasty thanks, opened the door into the hallway, and ran straight into Izzy Higginbottom.

NINETEEN

You know how you can tell someone is ticked off at you by the look in their eyes? That's how Izzy looked. But I was done playing by her rules. I had considered her a friend. A confidant. Someone who was on my side. Yet all along she'd known the truth about me and didn't say a word—and told Finn and Morgan not to say anything either. And let's not mention the whole lying to the entire town of Whitefall Cove. She opened her mouth, no doubt to berate me, but I beat her to the punch.

"Oh good. Just the person I wanted to see." My tone indicated my displeasure. My anger and hurt left an ugly taste in my mouth. "You and I need to talk." I was this close—this close!—to poking her in the shoulder with my finger. It was probably a good thing I still had Archie clutched to my chest, preventing me.

She flinched, then schooled her features. "Harper. What were you doing in the basement?" She used her headmistress's voice. In the past that voice would have intimidated me, but not today. Today I faced her as an adult on equal footing. I would not be cowed.

"I have some questions for you," I shot back, deliberately not answering her question, knowing it would annoy her. It did. Her spine stiffened and her mouth opened then closed several times. "Shall we go into your office?" I continued.

Not waiting for a response, I headed toward her office, heard her footsteps hurrying to catch up. She darted ahead of me and I could practically see the cogs turning in her head. She was wondering how much I knew, and how she could spin this so she'd come out of it golden. I was starting to see that was how Izzy Higginbottom operated. And let me tell you, the realization that someone you know, like, and trusted has taken a colossal fall from the pedestal you had them on? It is kinda soul-crushing.

She scurried around her desk and smoothed her hands down her suit before sitting, folding her hands and, with apparent calm, waiting for me to take my seat opposite. I did. Purely because I needed to sit down. My adrenaline rush was starting to decline. I could see what she was doing though, using her position as headmistress of Drixworths as a shield.

Her whole demeanor changed as soon as she slid behind the desk. I cocked my head, intrigued.

"You had no business going into the basement, Harper," she berated me.

"How long have you known I was a Whitelight Witch?" I asked, tone conversational rather than confrontational. Two could play at this game. And I learned from a master.

"What?" she squeaked.

"I know that you know." I nodded. "And I know that you told Finn and Morgan not to mention it. Have to say, Izzy, that stung. I'm wondering what the board of Drixworths would think of all this? You lying to the town and glamouring them to believe you? Lying to me about my magic." I made a tsk noise, shaking my head.

"I did it for their own good—for your own good," she protested, patches of red appearing on her cheeks. "I'm just trying to protect you all and you're turning it against me."

I sighed. "Actually I don't care anymore." It was true. I was hurt, yes, and annoyed and all of those things, but we had bigger problems. "I think you should call another town meeting and tell them the truth. About the rift. And that someone in this town is responsible."

"They'll panic!" she protested. "There'll be bedlam."

"You don't think people are panicking now? Have you stepped foot out of this place and seen what's going on out there? They think a demon killed Llewellyn. And they're scared they're going to be next. People armed with half-truths are likely to do stupid things." It was something I'd heard Izzy herself say before.

She deflated in front of me, the assured look on her face dissolving into panic. "I don't know what to do!" she cried. "I called in the experts to take care of this and now look. One of them is dead. The other two are constantly arguing in the basement and appear to be making no progress."

"My point exactly." I leaned forward. "Call a meeting. Tell the townsfolk exactly what's happening and ask for their help. We know someone living in Whitefall Cove is behind this. Yes, we risk tipping them off, but what if someone has noticed something dodgy about their neighbor? What if someone overheard something that they thought was odd, but not particularly important because all that's wrong—or so they think—is that our wards are broken and Finn and Morgan are going to fix those right up and all will be well again. If we all work together we can fix this. All Morgan and Finn need is to be able to pinpoint the person behind it. Once they have that, they can put a stop to the whole thing and close the rift."

I was still baffled why they couldn't get a trace on

who was dabbling in dark magic though. You would have thought it would have left a magic trail a mile wide. And while I had some answers from the duo downstairs, I wasn't entirely satisfied.

A commotion outside the door interrupted us and I spun in my chair when the door suddenly flung open and Gran appeared.

"Incoming!" she shouted. Archie, startled, shot off my lap, claws extended.

"What's going on?" I jumped to my feet, absently rubbing my thigh where Archie's claws had embedded themselves.

"Drixworths has been breached. Again." Gran huffed. "All hands on deck. We have a small army of trolls that need dealing with."

I shook my head. Trolls. I never, in my wildest dreams, thought I'd be battling trolls. Izzy ran past me and skidded out into the hallway, wand aloft, Gran hot on her heels. I paused in the doorway before turning back, spotting Archie under Izzy's desk. "Stay here, okay?" I told him, closing the door.

It was bedlam. At least twenty trolls were on the loose. Thankfully they were the dwarf variety and not giants, but they were vicious little beasts who could move surprisingly fast given their stumpy legs and squat bodies. Hurrying toward the front of the building, I was taken by surprise by one dropping over the staircase banister and landing on my back, its claws tearing through the skin on my shoulder.

"Son of a—" I snarled, spinning to try and dislodge the little beast, staggering under its weight and trying to dodge its other hand that was clawing at my face. Gran, hearing my yell, spun, spotted the troll and with a wave of her wand it was gone.

"Thanks." I puffed, my shoulder throbbing. But I didn't have time to check my injury or heal it, for a troll was heading Gran's way—make that two. Another had descended from the banister, leaping through the air with Gran in its sights, while the second one rushed her ankles. Shooting out both hands, I managed to obliterate them both.

"Stick with me," I grunted, rushing to her side. "Watch my back, I'll watch yours." We shuffled our way to the foyer, eyes peeled. Izzy was already there and besieged by the diminutive demons. With one on each leg and another on her back, she stood little chance of surviving their attack. I pushed my magic across the room and the trolls tumbled away, arms and legs flailing, but didn't disappear. I frowned. Was my magic failing?

"Everyone, gather in a circle, backs to each other," Gran hollered. Six witches and over a dozen trolls left to go. With us all in one place I used my magic to create a protective bubble, much like I'd done in the storm, although I knew it drained my energy fast. If I could protect us, the rest of the witches could dispatch them. Sucking in a breath, I pushed my magic out, surrounding us.

"What's that?" Dulcie, the purple-haired witch asked. "Is that a force field? Who's doing that?"

"Don't worry about who." Gran puffed. "Just zap the little bastards while we can."

The trolls ran toward us, hit the bubble and bounced away, rolling head over heels only to clamber back to their feet, scratch their heads in confusion, and try again. It would have been hilarious if it wasn't exhausting. Their constant attacks meant I had to keep reinforcing the bubble. Gritting my teeth, I channeled all of my energy into it. If I could hold it for a few more minutes we'd be done, and sure enough, we were.

"Finally!" Gran groaned, dropping her arm, her wand dangling limply from her fingers. "That was frickin' wild. How you doing, Harper?"

I dropped the shield, my legs like jelly. "Exhausted," I admitted, wobbling over to the staircase and sinking onto the stairs, afraid my legs would no longer hold me.

"It was Harper?" Dulcie asked, eyes wide. "I thought it must've been you, Izzy. Wow. You've got some skills there, Miss Harper."

Dulcie was in awe and I grinned. "Thanks."

"You're hurt." Gran touched my shoulder where

the fabric of my shirt was not only torn but also covered in blood.

"Can you heal me?" I asked. My magic was so depleted I doubted I could heal myself.

"Wait!" Izzy held out a hand. "Don't do anything. Not yet, at least. Anyone else here have an open wound? Did they break the skin?" The witches all checked themselves for injury.

"Me." A petite witch spoke up from the back and a path cleared as she made her way to my side. Ah. Petunia. I'd seen her around before but never really had much to do with her. She was such a tiny thing, so frail looking. She held out her leg, where three claw marks slowly oozed blood.

"Well done, the rest of you, for dodging those claws," I said, patting the step next to me in invitation for Petunia to join me. She did.

"You two have troll poison in your systems," Izzy informed us. I was glad I was sitting down for that one.

"What does that mean?" Petunia asked in her tiny voice. "Are we going to die?"

"Not at all," Izzy assured us, but given Izzy's propensity to lie to protect us, I wasn't one hundred percent sure she was telling the truth. Not in its entirety.

"What then?" I pressed.

"If we heal the wound with the poison still in you,

it means the wound will keep reoccurring and each time it will become more and more infected. And spread. We have to get the poison out first, then we can repair the skin and tissue damage."

"Okay, so how do we get the poison out?"

"A poultice. This is where Llewellyn would have come in handy," she added absently.

"That's a bit old school. Can't we draw the toxins out with magic?"

She shook her head. "Not if we want to get it all. I'm afraid it's going to be a slow process."

"How slow are we talking? Days? Weeks?"

"Oh no, not that slow. A few hours. Ladies, come with me to the gardens. Let's gather the herbs that we need. Alice, can you take Harper and Petunia to the infirmary?"

We did as instructed and it wasn't until I was sitting on one of the gurneys in Drixworths sickbay that something that had been staring me in the face suddenly became clear. "The wards."

"What about them?" Gran was having a good old nosey in the cupboards on the back wall while Petunia and I sat on the gurneys waiting for our poultices.

"Drixworths' wards. Why aren't they working? Is this place even warded? I mean, how are these creatures getting in? This is the second attack I've seen here, first gremlins—or was it goblins?—and now trolls? How are they getting in? This place should be warded up the wazoo."

"Good point." Petunia nodded in agreement. Gran paused in her rummaging and glanced at me over her shoulder. "I concur. A very good point."

"So the question is, are the wards broken? Or were there no wards to begin with?"

"We could ask Izzy?" Petunia said, but I shook my head. If there were a problem with the wards I highly doubted she'd be truthful about it.

"Gran? Could we ask the coven? Would they be able to check?"

"Child, I know a much easier way." Gran's grin was impish and I braced myself for what was coming. Whenever she got that expression on her face I knew it would be something I didn't like. "We'll just go ask Finn."

CHAPTER
TWENTY

Lying on the gurney, I stared at the ceiling and waited for Gran to return. Hopefully with Finn. Gran had been convinced he'd be able to help us and I didn't have the energy to argue. Nor did Petunia, if her light snores were anything to go by. In the distance I heard a door open, then close. I cocked an ear, waiting for the sound of footsteps, but nothing. Frowning, I slid from the gurney and tiptoed across the floor. Only one person I knew who moved without making a sound, and that was Morgan. Poking my head out the door, I caught a glimpse of her white gown as she rounded the corner, heading toward the front of the building. A second later the front doors of Drixworths opened, then closed.

Curious, I followed, ignoring the heavy weight of fatigue that dragged me down. Outside I caught a glimpse of dissipating magic dust, but no sign of Morgan. I took a few steps down the path, but she had disappeared and I wondered how she did it. Did she teleport? Or was she just lightning fast? Magic was definitely involved. I recognized the residual magic dust she'd left behind. She was the only supernatural I knew that did that.

Suddenly the earth tilted and I lost my footing. Falling to my knees, I winced at the sting as they hit the gravel, put my hands out to steady myself. Urgh, I felt so dizzy. My shoulder was throbbing and I belatedly realized I probably shouldn't have left the infirmary. Pushing myself back to my feet, I staggered to the front door, pushed it open, then fell back against it, glad for its support to keep me upright.

Where were Gran and Finn anyway? I knew Gran wouldn't dawdle, not when it came to my health, but it had been at least twenty minutes since she'd gone in search of Finn. And then Morgan had just snuck out. Although to be fair I'm not sure if I could call it sneaking, it was just the way she moved, gliding along as if her feet didn't touch the floor.

"Gran?" I croaked, cleared my throat and called louder. No answer. Which wasn't like Gran at all. I knew Finn was a big hunky guy who, under other circumstances, she would be all over, but not while I was ill and needed help. The second I was healed and back to full health she'd be flirting up a storm with him, I had no doubt. Staggering down the hallway, I made my way to the basement door, trying to stay upright as the walls dipped and swayed around me.

"Gran?" Throwing open the basement door, I slowly made my way down the stairs and into the basement, a strange muffled noise reaching my ears. What was that? After what felt like an eternity I reached the bottom, my eyes widening in disbelief at the sight that greeted me. Gran and Finn were tied together. I blinked, wondering if my vision was playing tricks on me, but nope, they were definitely tied together. More precisely, they were tied to chairs that were pushed back to back with another rope tied around their torsos.

"What's going on?" I stepped closer. Was this a trick? Or was I hallucinating? I'd never been poisoned by a troll before. Neither Gran nor Finn answered me, though they both swung their heads my way which was when I spied the duct tape covering their mouths.

"Far out," I muttered. Hurrying forward, I ripped off the tape, apologizing to them both when they winced at the unexpected facial waxing they'd just received. "Did Morgan do this?" I asked, tugging at the ropes, but they wouldn't budge.

"Magically reinforced," Finn said between clenched teeth, his anger palpable.

"How do I get them off?" If the ropes were secured

with magic, then how would my magic free them? Not that I had much, if anything, left to give.

"Inside my boot. A dagger. Use that to cut the ropes," Finn instructed me. Crouching in front of him, I slid my fingers inside his boot, blushing at the strangely intimate act. Curling my fingers around the handle, I pulled the blade free, careful not to scrape it against his skin.

"How you doing, love?" Gran asked. "You don't look so hot."

"I don't feel so hot." Bringing the blade up, I applied it to the ropes, sighing in relief when it cut through them like butter. I freed Finn first, who took the blade from me and made quick work of releasing Gran. By this point I was sitting on the ground, my legs unable to support me. My vision was starting to blur and darken at the edges and I let out a gasp of shock when I was suddenly scooped up and held against Finn's rock-hard chest.

"Easy." His voice rumbled in my ear and I didn't have the energy to argue. A part of me felt like I should muster up the energy to protest about being carried by him, but the other part won out—the part that was relieved beyond belief that I didn't have to get back to the infirmary under my own steam. Instead, I closed my eyes, lulled by the gentle jostling as he carried me up the basement stairs, down the hallway, and into the infirmary. I stirred when he laid me on the gurney.

"Petunia?" I turned my head to check on the other witch. She was exactly where I'd left her, sound asleep.

"Hold tight," Finn instructed, then tore the already ripped fabric away from my shoulder. Gran muscled in for a closer look, oohing and ahhing and telling me how gross my wound looked.

"Will it scar?" she asked Finn. "Tell me it will leave a scar. Not an ugly one. A cool one. A badass one. A warning to others not to mess with my granddaughter."

He chuckled. "It will not scar."

"Oh." She sounded disappointed.

"Stand back," Finn instructed, waiting while Gran shuffled backward a couple of steps. I braced myself, expecting the healing to hurt, but when he placed his hands directly on my injured shoulder, I felt nothing but warmth. And a little repulsion that he'd touched the torn up gashes. His big hands wrapped around the top of my shoulder, completely covering the injury. He looked down at me, lips curled in half a smile. "Won't take a sec." He told me. And sure enough, he removed his hands and I peered sideways at my ravaged shoulder only to discover it was healed. Amazed, I sat up, clutching the remnants of my blouse to my chest, touching the clear skin.

"Wow. I didn't feel a thing."

"If I do my job right, you shouldn't," Finn told me, crossing over to Petunia and repeating the process on her leg. She awoke with a yawn and a stretch and a sleepy smile at Finn. You could tell the exact moment when her brain woke up and she realized Finn Hurley was touching her. Her eyes widened and her cheeks filled with color.

I turned my attention to Gran, who'd whipped out her wand and set to work repairing my blouse. "What happened in the basement? I assume it was Morgan who tied the two of you up?"

Gran nodded. "That girl's got issues," she grumbled. "She's all white on the outside but dark on the inside."

Something clicked. "White..." I murmured. Morgan Healy was a stunning sorceress with pure white hair, dark skin, and wore long flowing white dresses. "She's a Whitelight Witch." It was what I'd thought all along, but everyone else had convinced me otherwise.

"What?" Gran snorted. "No, she's not. You are." But I was shaking my head. "You said it yourself. Although the Whitelight Witches are rare, it's highly probable that I'm not the only one."

"Just because you don't wear a lot of white and Morgan does, doesn't make her a Whitelight Witch," Gran pointed out.

"I'm not just talking about wardrobe choices. Ever since I returned to Whitefall Cove I've been told I'm powerful, that my magic is powerful. But no one could tell me why, or explain it. Then all this trouble starts and suddenly the name Whitelight Witch gets thrown around and then, boom, it's decided I'm it."

"Sounds reasonable to me. If it looks like a duck, quacks like a duck, chances are it's not a cat."

"I don't think I'm the only Whitelight Witch." I watched Finn as I said it, who'd been standing at the end of Petunia's gurney listening to our conversation. He turned his head and our eyes met. Did he know? Was he a part of it?

"What do we know of the Whitelight Witches anyway?" I continued. "A couple of fairy tales. And none of my special magical gifts appeared until after Llewellyn started training me."

"What are you saying?" Gran frowned. "That Llewellyn tricked you?"

I narrowed my eyes. "Not necessarily. Maybe I'm a Whitelight Witch, maybe I'm not, but what if you were a Whitelight Witch and wanted to keep that a secret for some reason? What better way than to point the finger at someone else, claim that they're a fabled Whitelight Witch? Don't you find it odd that suddenly at the age of thirty-one I gain the ability of telekinesis? That I can lift and move objects no matter how near or far away they are? That none of that showed up before now? Not even a hint?"

I couldn't believe we'd all fallen for it, hook, line, and sinker. My mind was a buzz. It was Llewellyn who had planted the seed of the Whitelight Witch—and he was close with Morgan. The passionate kiss that Gran had witnessed was a testament to that. Had they been working together? Too bad Llewellyn had gotten himself murdered. I sure had a ton of questions I'd like to ask him right about now. Like...why? Why this elaborate...hoax?

I glared at Finn. "Are you in on this?" Although his face didn't reveal much, he did have a slightly stunned look that he was doing a good job of hiding.

He shook his head. "What you say...has merit. But"—he held up a hand—"be assured that you are a Whitelight Witch, Harper."

"Could that be why you can't find the person responsible for the rift?" Gran suggested. "Because she's been right next to you this entire time? Blocking you."

"Do you think she's behind all of this?" I asked.

Finn lifted his shoulders, his face darkening. "I don't have answers to all of those questions, but I'm going to find out." The atmosphere in the room changed with his growing anger. I knew how he felt. I didn't like people messing with me either, but for someone like Finn, a powerful druid from the Otherworld, he wouldn't take kindly to being fooled.

"You said earlier that you knew I was a Whitelight Witch when you first arrived in Whitefall Cove," I said.

He nodded his head, a curt, abrupt gesture. "I did.

Although, that's not entirely true. It wasn't straightaway. It was the day after the town meeting. I could feel your magic on the edge of my senses." His eyes narrowed. "It was Morgan who suggested you may be a Whitelight Witch."

"And you probably didn't sense my magic until after I'd met Llewellyn for the first time." It was starting to become startlingly obvious that Llewellyn and Morgan were in on this together. Morgan had messed with Finn's perception of my magic, hoping to keep my particular brand of magic hidden, but when that hadn't worked she'd involved Llewellyn to suggest that I was a Whitelight Witch. At the same time, any hint of Whitelight magic could then be assumed to be coming from me, not her.

"Do you think she killed him?" It was the next logical thought. They were involved. They hooked up this scheme—whatever it was—together...and then what? Had a falling out and she killed him?

"I don't believe that, no," Finn surprised me by saying. "The way he was killed was mundane. And clumsy. If she wanted him dead she would have simply made him disappear." He snapped his fingers to demonstrate. "She could turn him into dust and he'd blow away on the breeze."

I gulped. That was powerful magic right there. And Finn was right. Even if Morgan wasn't a Whitelight Witch, she was still a powerful sorceress who most likely had a million different ways of getting rid of a body.

"Hang on, hang on." Gran waved her hands above her head and began pacing. "Lemme get this straight. We think—and let me stress that, right?— because we don't have any proof yet, but we think, Morgan is a Whitelight Witch. And for some god only knows reason, she and Llewellyn cooked up this hair-brained scheme to out Harper as a Whitelight Witch, therefore masking Morgan's connection to the White Lighters."

"Not sure they're called the White Lighters, Gran," I muttered. But Finn nodded anyway.

Gran continued, "But we don't think Morgan killed Llewellyn." We shook our heads. "And the rift? Is she behind that?" We both shrugged. "So really we ain't much further along than we were before."

I sighed. Gran was right. Why would Morgan open a portal to another dimension? Because if she was behind it, why hadn't she done anything with it? Other than having Whitefall Cove under constant attack from supernatural critters I thought were merely fairytales, to what end would she do this? It couldn't be power; she had plenty.

"I'll tell you what I think." Finn finally spoke. "We have two separate issues here." He held up a finger. "One, we have Morgan and Llewellyn and whatever they were trying to pull. And two"—he held up another finger—"we have whoever opened the rift."

"And where does Llewellyn's murder fit in?" I asked.

"Very good question." Finn frowned. "I don't know. Yet."

Seemed we were one step forward, two steps back.

CHAPTER
TWENTY-ONE

L earning I was not the only Whitelight Witch was a double-edged sword. On the one hand I was glad I wasn't the only one, the unique one, but the flip side was the possibility that I was sharing that spotlight with a psychopath.

"You okay, love?" Gran asked.

I smiled ruefully. "Yeah I'm fine. Let's go find Archie. I left him shut in Izzy's office." I glanced around. "Speaking of Izzy...where are they? They went to make poultices ages ago. I would have thought they'd be back by now."

"I'll go find them!" Petunia, who'd been listening intently to our conversation, slid off her gurney and headed out the door. Finn followed, muttering under his breath.

"Wait!" I called after him. "Something else has been puzzling me."

"What?" he barked and I jumped, startled at his tone. He immediately looked contrite. "Sorry," he apologized, rubbing a weary hand over his face. "This was meant to be a quick trip. An easy fix. Instead, everything is a shambles."

"Agreed." I nodded. "But just quickly, I was curious. How are these creatures getting past Drixworths' wards?" Even as I asked the question I was reasonably sure I already had the answer.

"Morgan," we said in unison.

Finn sighed. "I'll find Izzy and together we'll repair the wards. Morgan must have been working against us this entire time and I just didn't see it."

"She fooled us all." While it was true, it was also very little comfort.

"So," Gran said, rubbing her hands together, "what's next?"

"The way I see it, as Finn said, we have two problems. Possibly three. I say we let Finn deal with Morgan. None of us are strong enough to take her on and I don't fancy being turned into dust." I shivered at the thought. There was no doubting Morgan was a powerful sorceress in her own right, but add to that the fact that she was, we thought, a Whitelight Witch? Well, I didn't know what that meant, other than she was powerful and potentially dangerous. "I don't believe Morgan is behind the rift—she may be using it to her own benefit, but other than that I don't think she's involved, so I say we continue searching for whoever is—because I also think they're involved in Llewellyn's death."

Finn inclined his head. "Agreed."

"So...the murder club?" Gran grinned and I couldn't help but chuckle. She did love the murder club, there was no denying it. Slinging my arm around her shoulders I squeezed her. "The murder club."

We gathered at the bookstore, closing early due to the fact we'd had zero customers. The unrest in Whitefall Cove was bad for business and I winced when I thought of my bottom line. I had stock to purchase, wages to pay, and overheads to meet. I couldn't do that without customers.

I'd sent out a group text, calling the murder club to order and everyone had turned up, even Monica, despite it being daylight. She'd wrapped herself from head to toe, not a peek of skin visible. Gran had scurried across the road to Bean Me Up and returned carrying a tray with steaming cups of beverages. Jenna was there, as was Jackson, who'd taken one look at my face and pulled me into his arms for a prolonged hug.

"Thank you," I whispered, wrapping my arms around his waist. "I needed that."

"Thought so." He dropped a kiss on my head and held me for as long as I needed. Which was pretty much until everyone else started getting restless.

"Are we going to get started or what?" Gran grumbled. Reluctantly I pulled away, smoothing my hands down my thighs before using my magic to close the blinds and reveal the clue board.

"Right." I stood by the board and addressed the room. "Some developments I need to bring you up to speed on." I filled them in on what we knew, and what our plan was.

"So Finn is tackling the Morgan angle?" Jenna confirmed.

I nodded. "We initially called the murder club to order because of Llewellyn's murder—and despite him not being the person we thought he was— his investigation is still the reason we're here."

"Because you and Finn think that whoever killed him is behind the rift?" Monica asked.

"It's a possibility." It was all I had. A hunch. "We know Llewellyn was a player. A ladies man. I'm sorry, Monica, that's probably not what you wanted to hear."

She inclined her head ever so slightly. "I had no illusions. I wasn't looking for a happy ever after. I already told you, we were just having fun. So he was having fun with other women at the same time?

Doesn't bother me." I studied her intently, looking for signs that she was lying and found none. She'd come to terms with Llewellyn's actions and I was pleased for her. I wished I could be that blasé about it. It would bother me immensely if Jackson were seeing other women, let alone sleeping with them.

I pointed to the names on the board. "We know he was involved with Morgan. Possibly Vanessa Howe. As well as Monica."

"All women who, I would say, knew the score. Knew what they were getting into," Jackson said, casting Monica an apologetic look.

"So what you're saying," Jenna cut in, "is that you don't think his death was related to his propensity for sleeping around. You don't think any of these women killed him."

Jackson nodded. "Correct."

"That leaves us with the Oliver sisters." I tapped on their names. "And we have no motive for them."

"Other than the fact they bought a butt load of herbs from Llewellyn," Gran said.

"Wait, the tea shop ladies?" Jackson pointed to the board. To Gran, he said, "How do you know he sold them a butt load of herbs?"

Gran pulled a slim notebook from the massive tote bag at her feet, "Because he keeps a track of his inventory in here and it says so." She flicked through the pages until she found what she was looking for.

"They bought mandrake, nightshade, henbane, datura, hemlock, and vervain."

My eyes widened. "Those aren't for teas."

Gran was nodding. "I know. And he's got a note here, uxianna oil with a question mark. So maybe they requested the oil and he didn't have it?"

"Who else bought herbs from him?" Jackson asked.

"Simon Broughton bought Chelidonium—makes sense, that man's liver must be shot considering how much he drinks." She tskd, finger running down the page as she read the entries. "Carol Sharp bought some skullcap. She is high strung." Gran nodded. "I'd imagine that's to help with her stress."

"That's it?" I thought he would've sold more, but then he'd only been in town a few days.

"I'm more interested in what the tea shop ladies bought." Gran closed the book and tossed it on the table. "If I didn't know better I'd say those are the ingredients of a spell."

"Yes, but what spell?"

"A rift-opening one?" Monica drawled, but I was shaking my head.

"No—at least I don't think so? Gran? Thoughts?"

"Actually," Jenna began flipping through her phone, "I did find something on the Oliver sisters. Didn't think much of it at the time, but now it's got me thinking..." She quickly scanned her notes, then said. "There was a third sister. Brigit. Only she died."

"Brigit? Where's Whitney? Didn't she say that's what Poppy and Hetty were calling the poltergeist?" I looked around for any signs of my friendly ghost who liked to hang out in my bookstore, only there was no sign of her. Typical. Just when I needed her she was off having ghostly adventures.

"Well, I'll be damned." Gran was nodding to herself. "I've got it."

"What?" we all said.

"I bet those two idiots were trying to resurrect their dead sister. We said all along that this magic was dark. What's darker than resurrecting the dead? And those herbs? You'd need all of that and more for such a spell."

"You've seen a spell that can bring back the dead?" I was shocked.

"Doesn't hurt to keep abreast of what is happening in the dark arts," Gran said, "providing you don't act on it."

"Where? Where did you see this?" If Gran had seen it, then possibly the Oliver sisters had seen it too and she was right, they were summoning their sister from beyond the grave.

"Why, Drixworths of course. In the library." She rolled her eyes as if it were perfectly obvious. Which I guess it was.

"I wonder if that's why the wards aren't working

at Drixworths," I said to myself, "due to the dark magic originating there."

"They wouldn't have cast the spell there though," Gran pointed out.

"Hmmm. You're right. So, what did they do? Copy the spell?" I said.

"If it were me I would've just torn the page out of the book," Jenna said.

"Good point." I nodded. "Especially if you were in a hurry. Get in, get out."

"There are protections around the dark arts books," Gran said. "So I'd say the sisters found a way around them. And you're right, Jenna, I'd say they'd physically rip out the page they needed. Which means if we're right, there'll be a trail for us to follow."

I thought of Izzy. Did she know one of the dark arts books had been tampered with? I wasn't sure what to think anymore. Izzy had said she'd known I was a Whitelight Witch but she was acting in my best interests by not telling me. Yet all of this was happening right under her nose. How could she not have known what was happening?

"You need to poop, Harper?" Gran interrupted my thoughts.

"What? No!" I protested. Why would she ask such a thing?

"Oh." She waved a hand. "You just had a funny

look on your face. Thought you might be needing to—"

"Okay! Okay!" I stopped her before she could continue. "We get the picture, thank you. No, I do not need to poop. I was thinking."

"You need to change your thinking face then," Gran muttered and Monica sniggered.

"How would we follow the trail?" Jackson cut in.

"We'd need to go to Drixworths and find the right book," Gran replied. "Get an energy reading off it, and then, hopefully, it'll lead us to the missing page. Of course," she added, "this won't work at all if they didn't rip the page out."

Monica was shaking her head. "Y'all know where these two live, right? Why follow a trail when you can go straight to the source? No point in wasting time."

Jenna agreed. "She's got a point. It doesn't matter if they ripped a page out of a spellbook or not. What does matter is we find them, confirm that it's them behind all of this, and end it."

"How do we end it though? If it is them?" I asked. "Let's say they cast the spell to bring back Brigit—and let's say that an unexpected side effect is this tear between dimensions. How do we fix things?"

The four faces staring back at me remained blank. That's what I thought. None of us had a clue. Which left one option. Finn. Only he was busy tracking down Morgan and dealing with that mess.

"Here's what I think." I tapped my lip. "We confirm that the sisters are behind this. We have to be sneaky —we don't want them to know that we know. So we confirm. And then we go get Finn. I don't want to drag him into this without being one hundred percent sure Poppy and Hetty are responsible."

Jackson nodded and my heart fluttered in my chest. Having him here by my side made all the difference.

"We'll split into two teams," he said, taking charge. "Harper, you're with me. We'll check out the tea shop. Jenna and Gran, go check out their house. Monica—"

"I'll stay here," Monica cut in. "If we had the storm cover from yesterday I'd be able to cope, but not today. I'm not sizzling myself for those—"

"Got it," I interrupted. "You can coordinate from here. We'll keep you posted. And Gran? No heroics please."

Gran sniffed and studied her fingernails. "Can't promise anything."

I rolled my eyes. Why did I even bother?

CHAPTER
TWENTY-TWO

It was quiet out. I'd never seen the streets of Whitefall Cove so empty in the middle of the day.

"Everyone's rattled," Jackson said, wrapping my hand in his as we left The Dusty Attic and headed toward the Esplanade where The Tea Leaf was situated. Archie trotted behind us, not willing to let me out of his sight. He'd been distraught when we'd opened the door to Izzy's office, deep scratch marks in the back of the door where he'd tried to get out. I'd picked him up and hugged him, kept him tucked against me until we'd entered my bookstore and he'd been content enough to sit upon one of the reading chairs in the corner and watch proceedings. But as soon as we'd moved to leave he was hot on my heels.

Jackson pulled out his phone and hit speed dial with his thumb, refusing to let go of my hand.

"Yeah, Liliana, I need you to do something for me."

Oh great. Today had been an especially shitty day so far and now I got to listen to Jackson talk to his ex. Albeit from what I was hearing it was strictly business.

"What do we have on Brigit Oliver? She's the deceased sister of Poppy and Hetty Oliver. I want to know how she died, when she died, and anything else of interest. ASAP." He hung up without waiting for a reply.

We rounded the corner onto the Esplanade. I could see the tea shop, empty tables out front. "Looks like it's closed," I said as we approached.

"Makes sense. Half the shops are closed. Like I said, everyone is rattled. It's better they're home in their warded houses than out here anyway. Less chance of getting caught in the crossfire."

I paused. "You think there'll be crossfire?"

"I think they won't go down without a fight. I think if they've gotten this far undetected they'll have a certain degree of cockiness about them, a certain sense of power."

"So...you do think it's them?"

He stroked his chin. "Hard to think otherwise, but that's what we're doing here now. Looking for evidence." We'd drawn to a stop outside the store. Through the windows, I could see chairs stacked on top of tables. The lights were out and it was dim and quiet inside.

"I don't see anything untoward." I sighed.

Jackson squeezed my hand. "Not like they're going to be dancing around a cauldron singing and chanting in the middle of their store. Could be out back."

I grinned. Good point. Jackson raised his finger to his lips to warn me to keep quiet, then, with my hand still clasped in his, we crept down the side of the store. At the back was a parking space and a dumpster and nothing else. My shoulders slumped. Nothing. They weren't at the store, but then Jackson squeezed my hand to get my attention, and pointed. There. Behind the dumpster, was a light. We crept forward, peered behind it to see a narrow window.

"Basement," Jackson whispered. I nodded. We moved to the other side of the dumpster, and crouched down just in case they happened to glance up at the window and spot us. "I'm going to go unlock the back door," Jackson said into my ear. "Wait here."

I nodded again, watching as he crossed stealthily to the back door, climbed the two steps, then pulled something out of his back pocket. Bending, he inserted it into the lock, jiggled it around until it clicked. Then he slowly turned the door handle and motioned for me to join him. Archie weaved between his legs and shot inside first and I almost yelled after him to wait but managed to stop myself with a hand over my mouth.

Silently we slipped inside, leaving the door open behind us—in case a hasty retreat was necessary, I assumed.

Opposite the storeroom was another door with a strip of light showing beneath it. He paused by the door, pressed his ear to it to listen. After a minute he pulled away and slowly turned the knob. The door opened and we glanced at each other before sneaking inside. We were on a landing with a wooden staircase leading down into the basement. I reached out to hold Jackson's hand again when suddenly there was a thump and he tumbled down the stairs, head over heels.

"Jackson!" I cried, hurrying after him. He lay at the bottom of the stairs, not moving. As I skidded to my knees I registered the sound of the basement door closing and looked up to see Poppy standing at the top of the stairs. They must've heard us enter the store and she'd waited in the shadows to ambush us. Jackson groaned and I turned my attention back to him, only to have my head jerked painfully back by the hair.

"So nice of you to drop in," Hetty hissed, dragging me back across the floor by my hair. Reaching back, I grabbed hold of her wrists and tried to minimize the strain on my scalp. Poppy hurried down the stairs, grabbed hold of Jackson's wrist, and dragged him across the floor in the opposite direction. Good grief these women were strong. They may look frail, but it was certainly a case of looks being deceiving. I watched as Poppy tied Jackson to a post before stalking toward me, evil in her eyes.

"Tie her," Hetty hissed, letting go of my hair and kneeing me in the back as she did so, making me lose my balance. That's when I noticed it. A pentacle painted on the floor, in the center a wooden chair with leather straps on the arms and front legs. I gulped, an uneasy feeling settling over me.

"Look at her face." Poppy sniggered, tugging me toward the pentacle. Yep, it was as I suspected. That chair was meant for me. "She's figuring it out."

"Lemme see, lemme see." Hetty chortled and Poppy obliged, snatching my hair and wrenching my head around to face Hetty. My neck screamed in agony at the sudden, overextended movement. Gah, I had whiplash for sure. Which, in the whole scheme of things, was the least of my problems. Distracted by the pain in my neck, I missed my opportunity for escape and before I knew it, I was strapped in the chair. How had this happened? My eyes landed on Jackson, his hands tied to the pole behind his back, his head slumped on his chest. I watched it rise and fall and sent up a little prayer of thanks that he was at least still breathing, still alive.

Poppy hurried over to her sister's side and the two of them were busy at what had to be their altar, their backs to me.

I cleared my throat. "So I guess you two are behind all of this?" I asked. "The rift."

Hetty nodded, casting me a glance over her shoulder. "Not intentional, but a great distraction. Couldn't have planned it better if we tried."

"What is it you're planning?" All I could think of was to keep them talking. Hopefully, the others would be at their house by now and turn up empty-handed. When we missed our check-in with Monica they'd know something was up and come and rescue us. That was how I saw it panning out in my mind.

Poppy snorted. "Don't think we're stupid, Harper Jones."

"I don't think you're stupid." I shook my head. "Not at all."

"We're sure you've figured it out for yourself. After all, why else would you be sneaking around upstairs?"

"Fair enough," I conceded. "How about I tell you what I think and you can tell me if I'm right or not?"

Poppy cast a glance my way before turning her attention back to the altar.

"I think you're trying to resurrect your dead sister, Brigit," I said.

It sounded so fanciful, so melodramatic that it was an anticlimax when Hetty nodded and said, "Spot on."

"But...why?" I pressed.

"Uh duh. The power of three." Hetty snorted as if I was a simpleton. "If Brigit had kept her wits about her in the first place none of this would have happened."

"How did she die?" My mind was madly scrabbling to make sense of this. The power of three. What did that even mean? I wished Gran were here, she'd know, but I was also grateful she wasn't here. At least she was safe away from these two nutters.

"Stupid girl, fooling around with a vampire. No good ever comes from vampires," Poppy snarled.

"Vampires?" I frowned. Monica hadn't had any dealings with the Oliver sisters before, so that only left Vanessa Howe. Half-vampire, half-sorceress. "Oh. Did Brigit have her portrait painted?" I asked, knowing Vanessa required blood from her subjects. But only a pinprick of blood, nothing that would lead to your death.

"Oh, she had more than her portrait painted. The silly girl thought she was in love." Poppy clicked her tongue.

"What? With Vanessa?"

"What?" Poppy shot back then snorted. "No! Ewwww. One of Vanessa's friends from the city. Struss."

"Not Struss," Hetty said. "Straos."

"Straos? No...wasn't it Stravos?"

The two of them went back and forth over the vampire's name. It made little difference to me. I had no idea who he was.

"What happened then?" I interrupted them. "To Brigit?"

"What do you think happens to red-blooded females who run with vampires?" Hetty snapped, eyes narrowed in rage. "He killed her. Drained her dry in some sort of blood lust attack. Ravaged her to death."

"Is that why..." I cleared my throat. "Is that why you made Llewellyn's death look like a vampire attack? As payback?"

Poppy grinned. "It does have a sense of poetic justice about it, doesn't it? Of course, we realize we didn't quite pull it off. We expected someone to figure it out a lot sooner than you did."

"Kudos to us." Hetty chuckled with pride.

"Indeed." Poppy nodded.

"But we got what we needed." Hetty moved to indicate the mason jar on the altar. A mason jar full of red liquid. Llewellyn's blood, I presumed. My stomach rolled and I turned my gaze away.

"You needed all of his blood?" I queried.

"Not at all. Just a drop would have done." Poppy's smirk bordered on deranged.

"Yes, well. He shouldn't have laughed at us." Hetty pouted. "He thought it funny that we thought the poltergeist was Brigit. We had the last laugh."

Oh my god. That day that Whitney had witnessed Llewellyn setting the trap for the poltergeist. That had sealed his fate. Teasing the witches that their little ghost problem was not their sister playing tricks. I could see it now, how his teasing could be taken the wrong way. Especially by the Oliver sisters who were apparently unhinged.

"Yeah," I muttered under my breath, "you showed him."

"And now we have the last ingredient!" It was weird how they said that in perfect unison.

"What? Me? I'm an ingredient?" I blustered, tugging at the leather bindings clamping my wrists to the arms of the chair.

"Your magic is." Hetty headed toward me, a chalice in her hand. I didn't want to know what was in it. I suspected the herbs that Gran had read out earlier, plus Llewellyn's blood. Gross. Not to mention deadly.

"Open up." Poppy coaxed from the sidelines, picking up a black, leather-bound book from the altar. I blinked in surprise. They hadn't torn out a page of the spell book. They'd stolen the entire book!

I shook my head, clamping my lips together. I had more questions but knew better than to ask. The minute my lips parted Hetty would stuff the contents of the chalice in my mouth and I'd be screwed. It occurred to me, sitting tied to a chair and gripping my lips together so tightly they hurt, that Brigit might be requiring my body too. They'd need a vessel and what better way than to kill the witch whose magic you steal?

"You're going to have to give me a hand, Poppy," Hetty grumbled, standing in front of me. Too bad my legs were tied. I could have kicked the chalice out of her hands. As it was, all I could do was wiggle and jiggle and tug against my bonds. My magic was powerless within the confines of the pentagram, seems these two had thought of everything.

"Fine." Poppy huffed, placing the book back on the altar and coming up behind me. She wrapped her fingers in my hair, her nails digging painfully into my scalp, then she wrenched my head back. Of course, I opened my mouth on a yelp.

"Now!" she shouted. Hetty came at me with the chalice while simultaneously the basement door exploded inward. Next thing I knew Hetty was flying through the air and slamming into the wall. I sagged in relief when Finn casually made his way down the stairs, one hand outstretched toward Hetty, the other toward Poppy, both witches pinned against opposite walls.

"You okay?" he asked me, eyes running over me before turning to Jackson. I nodded. I needed to wee, but other than that, and the sore neck, and possibly a bald spot on the back of my head from all the hair pulling, I was fine. Archie came barreling down the stairs and leaped onto my lap.

"Did you rescue me, boy?" I asked. He bumped his head against me and purred.

With his magic holding the witches in place, Finn turned his attention to freeing me, then Jackson. "Yeah, your cat was tearing down the street as if the hounds of hell were after him," Finn said, placing a healing hand on Jackson's head. "Your friend Monica called me. I was already on my way, but your familiar led me the rest of the way."

"Oh, good boy," I cooed, hugging him to my chest.

Jackson stirred, blinked, then his eyes zeroed in on me. "Are you okay?" He was on his feet and by my side within seconds.

"I'm fine," I assured him. "I was more worried about you."

"I'm good." He turned to Finn and held out his hand. "Thank you." Finn shook hands, then looked at the two witches who'd not only murdered Llewellyn but opened a portal to another dimension in the process.

"Time these two paid the price of their crimes," he said. Using his magic, he herded them up the stairs and out of the basement. Jackson and I followed.

"I wonder what's going to happen to them?" I whispered.

"Nothing good," Jackson whispered back.

CHAPTER

TWENTY-THREE

After the dramatic takedown of Poppy and Hetty Oliver, the rest was anticlimactic, to say the least. Guards from Drixworths head office in East Dondure had arrived to take them into custody, the portal to the other dimension had been closed, not a single demon, troll, gremlin or goblin remained. Morgan had tricked us all—again. She'd led us away from Drixworths and we'd followed, only she'd doubled back and had used Finn's doorway to enter his realm. He'd been angry, wondering if that had been her intent all along. Lure him away from the doorway to the Otherworld, leaving it unguarded so she could slip through. He bid us a hasty farewell and had returned to the Otherworld, closing the doorway behind him, so even if she wanted to, Morgan couldn't return. Not to this exact time and place anyway.

We regrouped at The Dusty Attic to fill Monica in.

"So how did they do it? How did they overpower Llewellyn?" she asked.

"Get this!" Gran was busting to tell the story, so I leaned back against Jackson's chest and let her. "They knew you were sleeping with him. So they waited until you left his RV on the night in question, then Poppy spelled Hetty to look like you. It probably wouldn't have held up to a lot of scrutiny, hence catching him when he's vulnerable."

"As in... asleep." Monica nodded.

"Exactly. So he opens the door, all bleary-eyed and thinks it's you. Back for round two, you saucy minx." Gran winked at Monica. "Hetty convinces him to lie down and go back to sleep, which he does and then using a numbing spell. She punctures his wrist and begins to drain his blood. Meanwhile, she lets Poppy in and they have a merry old time searching his RV, but then he starts to wake up, starts to realize something is seriously wrong. Poppy slashes his wrist to hasten the blood loss. Then they take off. But Llewellyn wasn't quite dead. He's groggy from the blood loss, the wound is partially healed, but he'd lost too much blood to survive, magic or no magic. He staggers outside. Presumably to find help. And dies."

"Wow," Jenna muttered, hitting stop on the recording app on her phone. "I would never have suspected those two."

I opened my mouth to agree when my phone buzzed. Gran's did too. All Whitefall Cove witches were to present to Drixworths immediately for an urgent meeting.

"I guess we're in trouble." I sighed.

She grinned. "Only one way to find out."

"Sorry, guys. Looks like we'll have to catch up later," I said.

"Not a problem. Drop by Brewed Awakening this evening and we'll celebrate in style." Monica hugged me and I squeezed her tight, so happy she'd been cleared of this entire mess.

"I've got a story to write up anyway." Jenna grinned, throwing me a wink as she headed out the door. "Thanks for the scoop." I waved her off with a smile.

"I'll call you as soon as we're done," I promised Jackson, draping my arms around his neck and reaching up on tippy toes to kiss him.

"You'd better," he growled against my lips.

Then it was just me, Gran, and Archie. And two hundred other witches as we all converged on Drixworths Academy for Witches and Wizardry. We filed into the biggest classroom, which kept magically expanding to accommodate us all. Izzy pushed her way through the crowd to stand at the front of the classroom, her face pale, her hair disheveled. I'd never seen her look so...ungroomed.

"Witches and wizards!" she shouted. "Please, take a seat." We sat and silence descended.

"First of all, I want to thank everyone for their assistance during this unfortunate time in Whitefall Cove. We couldn't have done this without you." There were nods and murmurs and Izzy waited for silence again before continuing.

"But the truth of it is..." She swallowed and I frowned, noticing the tears in her eyes. "I failed. I failed you. I failed this town. I made some poor choices, some bad decisions, and they've had consequences." Her breath hitched on a sob and the tears fell, streaming silently down her cheeks.

I glanced at Gran, concerned. Izzy tried to get herself under control but when she opened and closed her mouth several times but was unable to speak past the emotion clogging her throat, we all started to look around, uncomfortable. What should we do?

"What Miss Higginbottom is trying to say." A male voice boomed from the back of the room. All heads swiveled toward Christian Alvarez, the head wizard from East Dondure—we should all recognize him, his portrait was in the foyer downstairs. "Is that she will no longer be continuing as headmistress of Whitefall Cove's branch of Drixworths Academy."

Startled gasps followed his words.

"Who will then?" Gran called out. Christian glanced at Gran. Then me.

"Very good question Alice Brewer." He inclined his head slightly. He knew Gran's name. I wasn't sure if that was a good thing or bad.

"I will oversee the school temporarily while a replacement is found. To that end, if any of you wish to apply for the position, you are welcome to do so. Please see me for an application form. Secondly, there will be some changes forthcoming and we will try and minimize any disruption to the students. Please. I invite you to give Miss Higginbottom a round of applause for her time here at Drixworths and join me in wishing her well for the future."

The room exploded in applause and Izzy managed to stop crying long enough to give us a watery smile.

"Didn't see that coming," I said to Gran.

"Nope." She nodded, then grinned. "I'm going to apply," she said.

"What? To be Drixworths next headmistress?" I snorted.

"Yep. It's going to be awesome." She sighed, a dreamy expression on her face.

Can you imagine? Alice Brewer, headmistress of Drixworths Academy of Witchcraft and Wizardry? Heaven help us all.

THE END

Ready to read Harper's next adventure in **Witch Way to Secrets & Sorcery***? Get your copy here:*
www.JaneHinchey.com/SecretsAndSorcery

Thank you for reading! If you enjoyed this book, I'd greatly appreciate your review.

You can find a complete list of my books, including series and reading order on my website at:

www.JaneHinchey.com

Join my newsletter here:

www.JaneHinchey.com/subscribe

And finally, join my readers group on Facebook here:

www.JaneHinchey.com/LittleDevils

Thank you so much for taking a chance and reading my book . It's readers like you who make this journey worthwhile and fuel my passion for storytelling. Your support means the world to me, and I can't wait to share more exciting stories with you in the future.

xoxo
Jane

FREE BOOK OFFER

Want to get an email alert when a new book is released?

Sign up for my newsletter today,

and as a bonus, receive a FREE e-book of

Cupcakes & Curses!

READ MORE BY JANE

Find them all at www.JaneHinchey.com/books

<u>The Ghost Detective Mysteries</u>

#1 Ghost Mortem

#2 Give up the Ghost

#3 The Ghost is Clear

#4 A Ghost of a Chance

#5 Here Ghost Nothing

#6 Who Ghost There?

#7 Wild Ghost Chase

#8 Easy Come, Easy Ghost

#9 Life Ghost On

<u>Witch Way Paranormal Cozy Mystery Series</u>

#1 Witch Way to Magic & Mayhem

#2 Witch Way to Romance & Ruin

#3 Witch Way Down Under

#4 Witch Way to Beauty & the Beach

#5 Witch Way to Death & Destruction

#6 Witch Way to Secrets & Sorcery

The Gravestone Mysteries

#1 Fur the Hex of it

#2 Battle of the Hexes

#3 What the Hex

The Midnight Chronicles

#1 One Minute to Midnight

#2 Two Minutes Past Midnight

#3 Third Strike of Midnight

Clean Scene Inc.

#1 All in Vein

PARANORMAL ROMANCE/URBAN FANTASY

The Awakening Trilogy

Hell's Angel Trilogy

The Enforcer Series (4 books)

Standalones

Returned

Secret Fates

Destiny's Touch

Blood Cursed

Heart of Darkness

ABOUT JANE

Hi there! I'm Jane, crafting tales of paranormal cozy mysteries sprinkled with urban fantasy romance. Between sips of coffee and dodging my mischievous cats, I immerse myself in stories where magic meets everyday life.

Once known as Zahra Stone in the world of steamy urban fantasy, I've now merged those fiery tales under the Jane Hinchey banner. Off the page you'll find me binging on true crime documentaries or sneaking in a Power Nap. Dive into my stories and join me on an enchanting journey!

Find me here: www.janehinchey.com

f facebook.com/janehincheyauthor
ⓞ instagram.com/janehincheyauthor
ⓐ amazon.com/Jane-Hinchey/e/B0193449MI
BB bookbub.com/authors/jane-hinchey
g goodreads.com/jane_hinchey